Rosanna and the Wizard-Robot

RACHEL BILLINGTON

Rosanna and the Wizard-Robot

Illustrated by Kate Mellor

METHUEN CHILDREN'S BOOKS · LONDON

First published in Great Britain by Methuen Children's Books Ltd.,
11 New Fetter Lane, London EC4P 4EE.
Copyright © 1981 by Rachel Billington
Illustrations copyright © Methuen Children's Books Ltd.
Set in 11pt Journal by 🅰 Tek-Art, Croydon, Surrey
Printed in Great Britain by
Butler & Tanner Ltd, Frome and London

British Library Cataloguing in Publication Data

Billington, Rachel
   Rosanna and the wizard-robot.
   I. Title   II. Mellor, Kate
   823' .914 [J]   PZ7

ISBN 0-416-21840-7

CONTENTS

For Nat, Rose, Chloe and Caspar

THE BEGINNING

One warm afternoon in May Rosanna came back from school feeling particularly energetic. She took off her convent boater with the striped ribbon and turned three somersaults on the end of her mother's bed.

'I'm bored,' she cried, when she'd finished. 'I'm so bored I may die.'

'Good,' said Zoe taking her two sucking fingers from her mouth. She was snuggling up to their mother, who was leaning against the pillows.

'Poor darling,' said her mother who was always more sympathetic when Rosanna first came back from school. In another half hour she'd scream at the very idea of somersaults on her bed. 'Why don't you go and have a swing in the garden?'

'If I die when I'm on the swing I'll fall off and hurt myself.'

'You can't hurt yourself if you're dead already.'

'Cats have nine lives.' Rosanna began to feel better. There was nothing she liked more than a good argument.

'You're not a cat.'

Surely her mother could do better than that. But before Rosanna could raise the tone, Zoe took her fingers out of her mouth again, 'I am!' she shouted triumphantly.

'You're a silly baby!' Rosanna shouted back. Zoe always reduced everything.

'Oh darling. Do go outside.'

She could see her mother's sympathy was already waning.

'Why doesn't Zoe have to go out?'

'She's tired.'

Rosanna picked up her boater and swung it round and round on the elastic. She hoped it would break but it didn't.

'I'm bored,' she said again. At that moment the boater flew from her hand and spun like a frisbee towards Zoe. It hit her with a crack on the arm. Zoe gave one of her train whistle yells.

'Rosanna! Now look what you've done!'

Zoe's screams came in a morse code. 'Aaaah, aaah, eeh! Aaah, eeh, aaaah!'

'If you'd gone down when I said this would never have happened.' Rosanna's mother's face had gone pink and Rosanna half hoped she would jump up and give her a smack. But she didn't. She hadn't jumped anywhere for months.

She stuck her fingers in her ears. 'I'm going. I'm going. I'm sorry. It was an unforeseen accident.' She started out to the landing. 'Can I have an apple?'

'On the kitchen table.'

'And a piece of cheese?'

'In the fridge. There's no need to make so much noise, Zoe. You're not dying.'

'I am. I am. I am!'

Under the circumstances, Rosanna was pleased to go into the peaceful garden. She sat on the swing with her apple and cheese.

The screams from her mother's bedroom died away soon. She imagined Zoe and her mother lying together half asleep on the bed. Her mother was expecting a baby and 'had problems'. She had to stay quiet in bed.

It was very warm. Rosanna leant back and looked at the blue sky with a few ragged white clouds. They seemed in a terrible hurry to get from one side of the sky to the other.

It must be windy. She looked down a little to the two big chestnut trees the other side of the fence. Their leaves were twirling round as if they wanted to twist right off the branches. Her side of the fence white blossom from an apple tree whirled down onto the grass like snow-flakes. A drift almost reached her where she sat. Along the garden wall bunches of mauve wistaria shook as if they were altar bells.

Even the flowers in the long flower-bed were waving about like rows of little flags. Rosanna amused herself choosing a flag for each country. 'Daisies for Denmark, Tulips for Turkey, Irises for India. Roses for Rumania. Bluebells for . . .' She hesitated. She thought there was a country called Bulgaria. But it might be Belgravia. Anyway now she had run out of names for flowers.

Despite the wind it was very quiet in the garden. It was odd that all the movement made no noise. A little creak from the swing sounded quite loud. She sat still. There was a slight rustling. Like her mother's petticoats when she went out to a party. Only she didn't go out to parties anymore. Rosanna loved parties.

11

Rosanna finished her apple and threw the core into a clump of pansies. Their round faces looked up at her reproachfully. Pansies for parties. And petticoats with real lace.

Cars and bicycles and aeroplanes didn't move any faster than the clouds or the leaves or the flowers but they made the most dreadful racket. They smelt horrid too. Inside and out. Rosanna was always car sick when they went for a trip. From where she sat the traffic on the main road sounded like the buzzing of a nice fat bumble bee.

Rosanna shut her eyes and began to swing gently backwards and forwards again. She hoped Mat wouldn't come home too soon. Mat was her older brother. It might be his day for Judo. He always went straight to his models and turned them all on. Some had three engines and made a remarkable amount of noise. They had special flashing lights too, so that he usually kept the curtains drawn in his bedroom. It made mama very cross. Particularly on a sunny day. If he didn't play with his models he watched television. Or practised the piano. Everything Mat did made a noise.

A boy at Rosanna's school had a train set. A train set might be quite nice. The boy was fat and bottom of the class. Rosanna was top of the class.

'It's extraordinary how sleepy a swing makes you,' she thought. 'I suppose Mary feels like this when I push her cradle.' Mary was a doll. Rosanna still liked dolls very much although she was seven and top of her class. It was a pity she hadn't brought out Mary. She liked sun and wind. Though strangely enough it was quite calm on the swing. She felt far too lazy to go and get her now.

THE QUEEN'S BEDROOM

A moment later an agitated tugging at her skirt made her open her eyes.

'Didn't you hear the bells? They've been ringing for ages.' An anxious piping voice spoke from near her knee. 'If you don't come soon I don't know what she'll think.'

'Who?' asked Rosanna, looking down, curiously.

'The Queen, of course.'

Rosanna found she was looking at the smallest and prettiest child she had ever seen. She can't have been much taller than a doll. She had silky chestnut hair, china blue eyes and a rosebud mouth, at the moment pursed with disapproval. Her dress was as pretty as her face. It was embroidered with yellow butterflies and pink flowers and showed a delightful scalloping of lace under the hem. Despite her curiosity in the idea of a queen, she couldn't help commenting on the dress first.

'I've never seen such a pretty dress in my life,' she said enviously. 'Are you going to a party?'

'That's hardly the point, is it?' The blue eyes became

14

quite fierce. 'Do you want me to tell the Queen you won't come.'

'What Queen?' asked Rosanna, thinking that the butterflies were remarkably life-like. They looked as if their wings were moving.

'I think the sun must have gone to your head. Our Queen. The Queen of Belgravia.'

'Oh,' said Rosanna stupidly. And then to show she was not ignorant added, 'I was admiring the Belgravian flag only a few minutes ago. Such a pretty blue.'

'You'll be black and blue, if you don't hurry. Loiter, loiter, loiter, you'll loiter your life away if you're not careful.'

Rosanna thought it odd to be addressed so sternly by a little girl who was really very like her doll Mary. However as she wanted to see the Queen and didn't fancy being turned black and blue she jumped up quickly.

'I'll run all the way!' she cried eagerly.

'You do exaggerate,' said the little girl who Rosanna decided she might as well call Mary as repeating 'the little girl' over and over again took up an awful lot of time.

'Do you mind if I call you Mary?'

'Not at all. Since it's my name. Now do mind the Queen's butterflies.' She moved forward as she spoke and was suddenly surrounded by a fluttering halo of butterflies.

'No wonder they looked so real!' Rosanna exclaimed. But Mary's dimpled bare feet were whisking away so fast that she had no time to wonder very long.

She soon found herself indoors and mounting a staircase carpeted with the thickest, reddest carpet

15

Rosanna had ever seen anywhere. Under normal circumstances she would have used it at once like a slide to bump all the way to the bottom. As it was she found it hard enough to keep up with Mary who disappeared round every bend before she could reach her. Luckily a stray butterfly usually hovered behind to guide her on.

She was quite out of breath by the time the stairs suddenly came out on a landing and she found herself face to face with Mary again. Well, knee to face. The landing was very wide and so bright that she felt almost dazzled.

'You'd better tidy yourself up,' Mary said in a disapproving voice.

Rosanna realised the landing was so bright because the floor which she had taken to be highly polished wood was actually a huge mirror. And the ceiling was pure glass so that the bright sky was reflected all around them. Unfortunately she could see herself too. Upside down. It made her feel sea-sick.

'I'm sorry,' she said humbly. 'It's my school uniform.'

'It's terribly dull.'

'I know. Although it's very expensive. At least this one came from the second-hand sale because my mother doesn't believe in spending money on children's clothes. Particularly ugly ones.'

'Ugly children?'

'Ugly clothes.' Rosanna was quite hurt as she was used to people thinking her pretty. She thought that a few butterflies might have cheered up her dress. But they had all returned to Mary's. She rather suspected they wouldn't want to exchange the pretty embroidered flowers for her plain blue gingham.

'Never mind,' said Mary sounding a bit more

sympathetic. 'The Queen might find you a cast-off. She has exquisite cast-offs. She once gave me a coat with a real fur collar. Now don't forget to kneel and kiss her hand.'

Rosanna saw that in one wall there was a huge golden door which as they approached slowly opened. A soft pink light wafted out carrying on its shimmering beams the most delicious scent.

'Roses,' murmured Rosanna.

'Don't be so self-centred,' whispered Mary over her shoulder. 'Actually its Gardenia with a touch of Mimosa. Rose is only for ordinary days.'

'Isn't today ordinary?'

'Extraordinary, stupid. Sshh!'

Now they were through the door pink light and scent was joined by a faint tinkling of music.

'Kneel,' whispered Mary. 'And then you may look. But don't forget about the kiss.'

Rosanna had been so distracted by the pink light and the scent and the music that she had quite forgotten about looking for the Queen. Now she did a quick bob like she did after Sunday mass and then opened her eyes as wide as she could.

'Oh! She's so beautiful!'

'Who's she? The cat's mother,' whispered Mary behind her.

'The Queen. She's like . . . she's like a . . .' Rosanna's voice tailed away as she tried to describe the magnificent figure at the other end of the room. She had a pale face but with pink cheeks and brilliant dark eyes. Black shiny ringlets were partly secured to the top of her head by glittering combs and pins and partly coiled round her shoulders. Layer upon layer of white and silver gauze draped around her arms and neck and then fell over the silkiest pinkest dress Rosanna had ever seen. Necklaces apparently made of stars and little pieces of rainbow fell nearly to her waist and then disappeared under the lightest softest looking rug Rosanna could imagine. It must be made by specially trained spiders, she thought. Amongst its glistening web, there was a continual play of bright colours which Rosanna realised were the butterflies from Mary's dress who had flown straight to the Queen the moment they entered the room.

'. . . like a, a . . .' continued Rosanna hopelessly.

'Queen, sweety-pops,' said a smiling voice.

'Kiss,' hissed Mary.

Bemused by the hiss and even more by the beautiful face calling her by such an unlikely name as 'sweety-pops' she stumbled forward. The scent grew stronger as she approached the draped throne-bed on which the Queen reclined. A delicate hand covered with rings that glowed like little candles appeared in front of her. She kissed it carefully, even remembering not to wipe her mouth afterwards because she knew that was rude.

'Now, Rosy-posy, entertain me!'

So she knew her name. Well her nick-name. That was nice. But the command to entertain was startling.

'Go on. Stand on your head. I like seeing people upside-down. It's so refreshing for the eye.'

'It makes me feel sick.' Rosanna was surprised into saying.

'Sick? How interesting. Perhaps you could do a handstand instead.'

'What I meant was it makes me sick to see me upside-down. Not to be upside-down.'

18

'But surely if you're upside-down, you seem the right side-up to yourself. It's only to people who stay the right-up-side-up that you seem upside-down. Otherwise one would have to be sorrier for the poor Australians than one is already. It would be awful to be in Australia *and* feeling sick.'

Rosanna wondered whether she should try and explain about the mirror-landing outside but decided on the whole it might be easier to simply stand on her head. She could do this easily.

'Oh, well done, honey-child!' The Queen clapped her hands. 'But what terrible knickers!'

Rosanna tried to pull her skirt over her knees which is very difficult when you're upside-down. She felt it would be too complicated to explain about gym knickers Monday, Wednesday and Fridays, upside-down so she let herself down. Then she thought it better not to explain at all. School could hardly interest this radiant vision. Not that she disliked school ordinarily. On the contrary. But as Mary had said this was an extraordinary day.

'What shall I do now?' she asked politely.

'Sing!'

'Anything?'

'Certainly not. Something wonderful.'

'Oh dear.' As Rosanna suspected, the Queen would clearly not be entertained by the usual school songs like 'I'm going to the zoo, how about you'. Perhaps a hymn might be best.

'Daily, daily sing to Mary

All my heart her praises due. . .'

She began rather quaveringly when the Queen interrupted her with a bejewelled hand waving.

'Isn't it rather tactless to sing to Mary? When you've got a queen here. After all, she *is* only a serving maid.'

'But it's not that Mary. . .' Rosanna tried to explain. 'It's Mary Mother of God. She's a Queen too. Queen of Heaven.'

'That's what I want a song for a Queen. Don't you know a song about a real Queen?'

Rosanna saw that the Queen was not quite as nice as she'd thought when she first saw her. Now she looked impatient and quite difficult to entertain. 'I know "God Save Our Queen",' she suggested doubtfully.

'Do you know the second and third verses?' snapped

the Queen so sharply that the butterflies rose in a cloud for a second before resettling.

'I'm afraid not.'

'As I suspected. I'm bored to tears of the first one. Everyone's always singing it to me. And standing up. So unsettling. I much prefer people kneeling. Oh, oh. I feel quite exhausted!'

With these words the Queen sank back into a pile of pillows behind her and closed her eyes. As the pillows depressed a soft cooing like pigeons in the trees made Rosanna wonder if they were stuffed with live birds instead of feathers like at home.

'You can relax for a moment,' said Mary. 'She's asleep. But don't do anything sudden.'

Rosanna was far too overawed to do anything at all. However she did take the opportunity to look round the room and note a few more details. The music, she saw was coming from an old-fashioned gramophone with a large golden horn. It had become very quiet now the Queen was sleeping. The tinkling piano had changed to a harp.

'What pretty music!' she whispered to Mary.

'Quite pleasant,' agreed Mary indifferently, 'though the musicians complain about the crowding and the heat.'

'Do you mean they're inside the gramophone?' exclaimed Rosanna, quite shocked.

'Of course.'

'They must be very small.'

'Of course,' repeated Mary, 'I'm surprised you don't admire the flower arrangements.'

Rosanna looked away from the gramophone, glad to be diverted from the sufferings of the inmates. Perhaps they were very very small. The flowers on the other hand were very very big. There were four main arrangements standing in sort of trays on top of four gilded tables. Indeed she had never seen such beautiful arrangements. The face of every flower was perfectly visible like people lined up for a photograph. When she thought how hard she found it to make three daffodils stand up in a vase it quite took her breath away.

'They're more like ballet dancers,' she said. 'I was once taken to Sleeping Beauty and they posed just like that.'

'It's not surprising with all the trouble they take. Hours before the Queen wakes, between the dawn chorus and the sunrise, they're posturing and posing. You'd hardly believe the fights that go on for the centre spot or failing that the front line. It's lucky they can't speak or the Queen would never sleep through it.'

'Do you mean they're alive?' gasped Rosanna, staring at the flowers which she now saw were indeed growing out of a layer of earth.

'Sshh. They're not deaf you know. And they're dreadfully sensitive to criticism. Dead flowers wouldn't be very pretty, would they?'

'No, I meant. . .' But looking at Mary's surprised china blue eyes she thought it better not to try and explain. It was humiliating to be constantly underestimated by a doll.

'You can sit on that cushion if you like,' Mary pointed to a red satin cushion with silver tassels. 'Get your breath before the Queen wakes and needs more entertainment.'

The large cushion lay under a huge open window to the right of the bed. Rosanna started to tip-toe towards it doing her best not to wake the Queen for the prospect of further entertainment was distinctly unnerving.

On either side of the window pale gauzy curtains blew in and out. Their frilly ends curled towards her like beckoning fingers. As Rosanna neared them she peered curiously through the window but although the sill was quite low she could see nothing except a bright blue sky glowing with sunshine and occasionally spotted by fast-moving white clouds.

She had just turned her back on this view to sit down when she felt a sudden rush of wind, something soft brushed over the top of her head and an ear-splitting screech pierced the calm.

THE CHERUB

Out of the corner of her eye she saw Mary's horror-struck face as she fled from the room. Then her attention was completely taken up by the extraordinary sight in front of her.

Hovering over the bed, about the size of a large sofa, was a white puffy cloud. It was clearly one of the ones she had seen speeding across the sky, which had now turned off course, brushed over her head and entered the room.

If a cloud alone wasn't enough, sitting in the middle of it was a naked cherub with golden curls. The noise was coming from a shining trumpet which she was blowing with all her might. Rosanna who was a member of the school orchestra thought that the cherub should have taken a few lessons before she blew quite so hard. It wasn't anything near a tune, just a dreadful screeching sound.

She looked nervously at the Queen and was quite surprised to see that her eyelids were only just fluttering. She'd assumed she'd be sitting upright with terror or fury. But except for that slight sign of waking she looked as peaceful as ever. Even the butterflies were only flapping their wings lazily.

Rosanna looked back at the cherub. It was true that apart from the horrible noise she was making, she would be hardly likely to inspire fear. She was so pink and plump and dimpled. Just the kind of creature grown-ups cuddled and said 'How sweet!' The way her cheeks and her eyes were popping out with all that blowing was really quite ridiculous.

'Darling angel, do you have to announce your presence quite so convincingly?' The Queen, leaning forward from her pillows (which definitely twittered as she left them) spoke reprovingly, though Rosanna noticed she had the equivalent of a 'How sweet' smile.

The cherub took the trumpet out of her mouth. 'Yes!' she said firmly before returning it and blowing again, this time in a series of short bursts.

'I hope there's nothing wrong,' said the Queen without raising her voice, 'Why don't you get off that nasty damp cloud and tell me all about it?'

'Oh, alright,' said the cherub bouncing up and down

25

on the cloud, just as if it was a trampoline. 'On your marks, get set, Go!'

As she jumped Rosanna noticed with some jealousy the neatest little gilded wings growing from her back. They flapped busily as she flew to the Queen.

'First of all,' said the Queen, 'I'd better make introductions. This is my darling little cherub, Zoe.'

'Oh' exclaimed Rosanna surprised and yet not surprised by the familiar name. The cherub giggled and was given a severe look by the Queen.

'And this is Rosanna who can be quite entertaining when she tries even though she wears horrible knickers and doesn't know the second and third verses of "God Save Our Queen". Not that I hold either thing against her. Knickers can always be changed and verses can be learnt.'

'I'm very good at learning things by heart,' said Rosanna eager to show off in front of the cherub. 'Shall I recite the school song or the leaders of the Trades Union or the last ten Popes? I can do the Popes backwards.'

'No thank you, sugar-pot,' said the Queen hastily. 'Though it's very kind of you to offer. We've got to find out why the sweet cherub was making such a noise with her trumpet first.'

The Queen and Rosanna both looked expectantly at Zoe who was sucking a curl. Becoming self-conscious under their gaze she crossed her little fat legs at the ankles and wriggled her toes.

'Well?' said the Queen quite severely.

Removing the curl carefully, the cherub opened her mouth very wide and then her eyes. There was a pause.

'Well?'

'I've forgotten,' the little red mouth closed shut and smiled sweetly.

'Oh really!' Rosanna couldn't resist exclaiming, 'You can't be as silly as that.'

'I can!' said the cherub.

'I'm afraid she can,' sighed the Queen. 'She's forgotten more things than anyone else has even tried to remember.'

'Not anyone surely,' said Rosanna, 'not a very very old person.'

She was interrupted by Zoe opening her mouth again and shouting, 'On your marks, Get Set, Go! I've remembered. I've remembered! It's all about Kitty. She's gone. No-one knows where she is. She's not under the pillow, she's not under the bed. She's not in her bedroom, anywhere. She's not even downstairs. She's gone. Poor Kitty. Oh, poor poor Kitty. She must be so lonely.'

Two huge tears appeared in Zoe's eyes and perched on the rim of her round cheeks. Rosanna noticed that the harp music had changed to a kind of wailing pipe sound.

'There, there,' said the Queen patting the cherub's hand. 'Think how lucky Kitty is to have you remembering all that.'

'Is it Cousin Kitty?' asked Rosanna curiously.

'Everyone is a cousin to someone,' said the Queen tartly.

It could have been a cat, Kitty, thought Rosanna, with all that talk of not under beds. But she decided not to comment out loud because the anxiety of Kitty's disappearance seemed to be having a remarkable effect on the Queen.

All the colour had gone from her cheeks and the curls in her hair were unrolling till it was only just wavy. While her glowing pink dress had changed to quite a gloomy mauve. Even the light in the room had gone a dim pearl colour which made Rosanna realise that the glowing pink before had come from the Queen herself. She obviously took Kitty's disappearance very seriously indeed.

'Can I help!' cried Rosanna jumping up and coming to the edge of the bed. 'I'm very good at looking for things.' This was true. Besides she was very fond of her cousin Kitty — if it was her cousin Kitty — and didn't at all like to see the glow go out of the Queen. Even the light from the window was darkening to a twilight pale.

'Oh, rootytoot!' said the Queen sadly. A snore came from near her elbow where the cherub had crawled under the bed-clothes and fallen asleep. No use in an emergency, thought Rosanna scornfully.

'You might begin by shoving the cloud out of the window. If we're not careful it'll start to rain. Clouds are terribly sensitive to atmosphere, you know.'

She had hardly finished speaking when there was a light pattering on the gauzy bedspread. A wave of butterflies rose indignantly.

'I told you so,' said the Queen. 'Quick. Before it really pours!'

Rosanna who thought she was rather good at getting unwelcome things out of windows — flies and swansdown and autumn leaves — found a cloud was a very different proposition. Wherever she tried to grasp it came away in her hand so that very soon the room was filled with little fluffy pieces of cloud.

'Never mind,' said the Queen calmly as Rosanna got

more and more hot and bothered. 'At least you've taken its mind off raining.' And Rosanna realised that indeed there'd been no more pattering for quite some time.

'Just push a few bits over the flowers in case and then leave it for now. They'll all go of their own accord in a minute or two.'

'Where?' panted Rosanna.

'To the horizon, of course. Clouds always gather on the horizon at the end of a nice sunny day. Now bring that mirror from the dressing table and we'll see where poor dear Kitty's got to. Such a good sweet girl.'

Obediently Rosanna first manoeuvred a few appropriate sized clouds over the trays of flowers who bowed their heads graciously as if in thanks and then went to a little dressing-table in the corner of the room. She had not noticed it before though she presumed it had stood there all the time. It was garlanded with long necklaces some made of silver, some of pearls, some of shells and some of all three.

'And do put on some necklaces while you're there,' called the Queen. 'We can't have you looking like a kitchen table-cloth all the time. Take at least six. Personally, I think anyone wearing less than six necklaces might just as well not have bothered.'

'Oh, thank you,' breathed Rosanna, putting the necklaces over her head one by one and staring at herself admiringly in the mirror. She looked like a princess, at least.

'And now the mirror,' commanded the Queen. 'The hand mirror. I hope you're not a vain sort of girl. If you are you'll find the necklaces turn into shoe-laces before you can say "princess". They do like credit to go

29

where credit is due.'

Rosanna hurriedly stopped smiling at her face and brought the pretty shell-backed mirror to the Queen.

'Oh dear,' she cried out instantly. 'What it is to have enemies. It's perfectly clear to me they've taken the dear child entirely to spite me. We must summon the Chief Wizard immediately. Where has that Mary gone to? Dolls are very unreliable when there's trouble, you know. See if she's outside the door. Though I wouldn't be surprised if she hadn't made a bee-line for her cradle. It's very difficult to persuade dolls to grow up at the best of times.'

Rosanna made her way to the door which was not as easy as it sounds for the clouds had started a slow progression out of the window and she kept losing her head in soft grey wetness. However eventually she arrived just in time to see Mary herself coming in.

'Oh, dear,' she began immediately, 'I suppose you want the Chief Wizard.'

'Of course I want the Chief Wizard. What's the point of having a Chief Wizard if you can't want him.'

'You can want him but can you have him?' mumbled Mary, just loudly enough for the Queen to sit up with a jerk.

'What did you say?' she boomed and this time the butterflies rose in a phalanx and streamed out through the window.

'I said the Chief Wizard says he's in the middle of a very important experiment and mustn't be disturbed.'

'Disturbed! Disturbed! Disturb him at once or I'll pull out all the plugs and then, where will his precious experiments be!'

Rosanna had never seen the Queen so nearly out of

her bed and found it quite a frightening spectacle. Her dress had deepened to a shiny purplish-black and her hair had coiled up again and was bouncing round her face like snakes. Rosanna was sure she could see yellow eyes gleaming at the curls' ends. The skin of the Queen's face and hands had become so pale that in the darkening room it seemed to be giving off an unearthly silver light. From the gramophone came an awkward squeaking and scratching.

'Isn't that "modern music"?' asked Rosanna trying to reassure herself by her cleverness but Mary only gave her a blank china look and went out of the room again while the Queen fell back against the pillows where she lay, statue-like, amidst a soft hissing.

'They must be snakes,' thought Rosanna nervously and went back to her place on the red silk cushion. It was quite cold as the night air came through the open window but she was far too frightened to close it. She wished she was the little cherub who was still fast asleep under the covers. She even wished for a moment she wasn't in the room at all until she was struck by the cheering realisation that she hadn't been bored for ages.

She was wondering whether to try and improve the Queen's mood with this interesting thought when a very weird thing began happening in front of her. It was as if a huge mole was trying to come up through the Queen's bed. When it couldn't get through in one place, it tried another. Rosanna watched, mesmerised.

'Honestly!' exclaimed the Queen, making her jump, 'if I've told him once to use the door, I've told him a . . .'

She never finished her sentence because the mole or whatever it was suddenly found an opening and shot to the surface. The only trouble was that the opening he found was directly under the Queen so that as he broke for air he shot the Queen up to the ceiling like a black and silver meteor. She hung there for a moment, her gauzy silver drapes trailing nearly to the bed and then gracefully floated back into her usual regal position.

'. . . I've told him a million times,' she finished calmly. Rosanna shut her mouth which had fallen open like a fish with the shock of it all and looked for the mole.

It was not a mole. It was a wizard. He stood on the bed with a tall pointed hat, a wand and a cloak made up of dozens of coloured lights flashing on and off. As well as the little clicks made by the lights automation he also emitted strange mechanical purrings and rumblings and squeakings. In fact he seemed to be something between a wizard and a robot. His voice, however, sounded quite normal, if rather loud.

'I'm sorry about that little miscalculation,' he was saying without sounding at all sorry. Actually he sounded excited and pleased with himself. 'But it's all your own fault for having such a tough bedspread.'

'My spiders spin the toughest webs in Belgravia,' said the Queen, apparently quite unruffled by what Rosanna would have thought to be a very ruffling experience. 'If they didn't I'd have them replaced by silkworms instantly. There's been a lot of union agitation about it as it is.'

'Yes. Yes!' cried the wizard-robot impatiently. 'The point is you've just witnessed a tremendous break-through . . .'

'Eventual break-through,' interposed the Queen.

'. . . breakthrough with my new Man-launching-pad

WX 1000. Do you realise I came from my invention chamber to here in .00003 seconds. And if it hadn't been for those stupid spiders it would have been considerably less.'

'I'm glad you're in such a good mood,' the Queen said with surprising patience, 'because Rosanna and I have a problem.'

'Rosanna?' asked the wizard-robot and looking round apparently saw her for the first time. 'Oh, hello,' he said in a less than enthusiastic voice. 'You look like a girl.'

'Of course I'm a girl,' she began indignantly but the Queen waved her hand soothingly.

'Don't take that personally. He's just more interested in objects than people so he's always hopeful that the human form covers an engine. As you see he's nearly managed to turn himself into a machine. He can be quite useful in emergencies.'

While they were talking the wizard (now that Rosanna was more used to his odd appearance she noticed he had dark brown eyes just like her brother Mat's) was flicking switches up and down and round and round all over his body so that not one part of him was still or silent for a moment.

'So what's the problem?' he asked when they were talking. Rosanna could see that he was the sort of person who didn't listen to what other people were saying, unless they were giving him factual information.

'It's poor dear Kitty,' said the Queen, 'she's been kidnapped. By the Washers, if my mirror's not mistaken.'

'Let's have some light on the subject,' said the wizard, looking more stimulated by the sad news than saddened.

Rosanna thought the Washers sounded terrifying. She pictured something between those dreadful green furry

33

things that threatened to squash her father's car in the garage and the pincer-like fingers of her mother when she washed her hair.

Meanwhile the wizard-robot had flicked various switches on his person and soon the room was flooded with a nice orange glow. 'Remote control,' he explained grandly in Rosanna's direction. 'I don't suppose you even know what the term means let alone how it works.'

'Oh yes, I do,' she said crossly, 'I'm not as stupid as you think.'

'No she isn't Mat dear,' said the Queen mildly. 'She can be quite entertaining even though she doesn't know the second and third verses of "God Save Our Queen".'

Rosanna noticed the wizard had stopped listening again but even so wished the Queen wouldn't go on about those verses. She promised herself to learn them the moment she had the opportunity. She thought they might be in the school song book.

'I'm top of my form,' she announced in self-defence.

'We'll begin by forming a telepathic link with the girl,' said the wizard who naturally hadn't heard her boast.

'You are clever!' said the Queen, giving him far too much admiration for Rosanna's liking. 'And how will you do that?'

'First, I shall have to return to my invention chamber . . .'

'Do use the door this time, darling.'

'. . . and then I shall need an assistant.'

'That's easy. You can have Rosanna. If I had to describe her I'd say she was the perfect magician's assistant. You don't mind terribly leaving the necklaces behind you when you go, do you, my petal? His invention chamber's so dirty and smelly. Besides he tends to take things to pieces to make them into other things, if you know what I mean. And I wouldn't want my pretty necklaces to end up as part of a transistorised communication module — however useful.'

Rosanna wasn't at all sure she wanted to leave what now seemed the relative security of the Queen's bedroom for some unsavoury and possibly dangerous dungeon and was just about to open her mouth to say so when a voice piped up from the bed.

'I want to be an assistant!'

The cherub's face appeared over the top of the bed-clothes. It was flushed with sleep and determination.

Rosanna immediately decided she did want to go after all. 'I'm ready,' she cried. 'How do we get down?'

'Easy-peasy!' shouted the wizard. He had to shout because the little cherub was screaming, 'I want to go! I want to go!' over and over again in the most babyish fashion.

'Just grip that yellow button on my left wrist and when I say, "kinhcet-rehcsif" hold your breath and jump.'

'Jump where?'

'Don't be silly. Just jump.'

THE WIZARD'S CHAMBER

Jumping with the wizard-robot was not at all like jumping in the garden or in the playground or even off the high part of the wall. It was most like jumping upwards on a trampoline, very high and without much effort and then coming down in a very fast lift. On the downward journey Rosanna was quite frightened of hitting the Queen's bedroom floor and as it became clear that one had somehow dematerialised, the floor after that and the floor after that. But in fact their smooth descent continued for what seemed a long time quite uninterrupted.

She even had the opportunity to wonder whether the wizard had simply opened a trap door into an elevator below the bedroom. But before she could ask him, they had reached the bottom of whatever they were in and she found herself flat on her face in pitch darkness.

'Crash landing, I'm afraid,' said a nonchalant voice beside her. 'But not at all bad otherwise. .00275 seconds. Not a record but perfectly respectable. And of course there were two of us.'

'Surely a heavier weight should come down faster,' said Rosanna, recovering herself although she did find the darkness off-putting.

'You know the Queen might be right. You could be good assistant material. At very least our greater weight could explain the crash landing. You're not hurt, I hope?'

'No. But I would like to see where we are, if it's at all possible.' Despite his approval Rosanna thought it wise to treat the wizard carefully.

'It is dark,' agreed the wizard as if he'd only just noticed it. 'Stay where you are while I find the switch.'

He moved away and almost immediately there was the most terrible clangings and clatterings. Rosanna knelt up in fear but as the noise was accompanied by 'Owhs' and 'Oohs' of mixed pain and annoyance she soon realised it simply reflected the wizard's progress through a very cluttered invention chamber.

'Can I help?' she asked bravely, as what sounded like a chain fell from a great height and only just missed her head.

'No problem!' came back the cheerful shout. 'Can't be a magician in these days of automation without a fair amount of equipment.'

'No I suppose not,' said Rosanna politely although she couldn't help thinking nostalgically of cauldrons and books of spells.

'Here we are. Kinhcet-rehcsif!' As Mat called out the magic words, there was a brilliant flash, a shattering explosion and the room round Rosanna roared into glare, movement, noise. On one side a huge cartwheel spun round with yellow and purple lights. On another a vast mechanical shovel scooped up flashing stones from a hole in the ground which it emptied onto a conveyor belt travelling upwards with much grumbling and creaking to some unseen destination. In another corner three weird mushroom shaped objects, with silver sparks shooting out of their dome heads, bounced on giant springs. The squeaking as they landed was particularly ear-splitting. In front of them a row of shining tubes filled with different coloured liquids passed backwards and forwards as if dragged by some kind of engine. At least their movement was accompanied by an odd puffing sound as Rosanna imagined old-fashioned steam trains used to make. Just behind where she sat a series of pistons to which were attached horrid life-like hands, except that each nail glittered with at least 100 watts, came uncomfortably close to snatching Rosanna's hair. Nervously she stood up, and moved out of range.

This enabled her to see a whole row of screens, not unlike ordinary television screens except that they were very small and had red and blue and green fronts instead of the usual grey. Hundreds of shining wires came bursting out of their backs and climbed up into the roof rather, thought Rosanna, as if they were plants looking for the sun. Although the screens were blank, a multitude of knobs on a giant control panel beneath them buzzed loudly and every now and again popped in and out.

'Not bad,' said the wizard proudly, 'not bad for a couple of days' work is it?'

'A couple of days' work!' gasped Rosanna, truly amazed.

'I scrap everything every third day. Too boring otherwise.'

'I feel as if I was,' began Rosanna slowly, 'standing in the middle of a fairground in the middle of a roundabout.'

'Humm,' said the wizard, not sounding too pleased at the analogy. 'Unsophisticated things, roundabouts. The engines could be run by a child with a pin and a rubber band. We've got more ambitious plans afoot.'

'Oh yes!' agreed Rosanna placatingly.

'Have you ever worked a telepathic visio-auro communicating machine before?'

'What?' said Rosanna pretending she couldn't hear him above all the machines though really she hadn't a clue what he was talking about.

'Never mind. Mind your head.'

Rosanna only just ducked in time as a huge round object something like a microphone but more like a bomb descended at speed from the ceiling. It hung in front of them bleeping slightly.

'Will it explode?'

'I knew you were a girl!'

'Sorry.'

'Now this is the programme. I stand by the screens and work the controls. You stand by the microphone and, after putting yourself into a telepathic communicative trance situation, speak Kitty's name loudly and clearly. Understood?'

'Yes,' said Rosanna, having no idea what a 'telepathic communicative trance situation' was but being fairly sure she could say 'Kitty' loudly and clearly even under such difficult conditions.

'Roger!' cried out the wizard enthusiastically and as he took up position by the control panel Rosanna noticed that his own lights which had been relatively dim were flashing on and off like over-excited traffic lights. 'When I say the magic words, press that gold button on the edge of the mike, concentrate tangentially for 30 seconds, concentrate centrifugally for 15 seconds, and then enunciate the girl's name as slowly as possible.'

'Roger,' echoed Rosanna with anything but confidence.

The wizard took a deep breath, twiddled several knobs and then shouted out, 'Kinhcet-rechsif!'

Rosanna also took a deep breath and then pressed the gold button. Having no idea what concentrating tangentially or even centrifugally meant, she was about to start a forty-five second count-down to Kitty's name when there was a huge explosion not unlike the one that had flung the invention chamber into action. It was followed by total blackness and silence.

'Mechanical mocking-birds!' exclaimed the wizard, his voice sounding very cross and loud, in the still darkness. 'A fuse! I suppose you pressed the wrong button.'

'No, I did not!' cried out Rosanna indignantly.

'Oh, well. Perhaps not,' said the wizard sounding a little less cross. 'Actually a fuse is no real problem, I invented a patent fuse reactor directive only yesterday. Quite glad to have the opportunity of trying it out as a matter of fact. You stay where you are, while I try and put my finger on it.'

Rosanna who had no intention of moving now she knew with what dangers she was surrounded listened as the wizard made his usual banging clattering progress across the invention chamber.

After a surprisingly short time there was a click and the room burst into life once more. The wizard-robot was revealed beaming broadly. 'It's almost worth a break-down to show off the efficiency of the normal service resumption programme.'

'Well done,' said Rosanna smiling too though she found his use of long words becoming a serious barrier to conversation. She half wondered if he didn't make them up to impress but that seemed rather a mean thought when he was trying so hard. 'Shall I press the button again?'

'Naturally.'

This time there was no explosion and Rosanna was able to recite to herself calmly, '45, 44 . . . 33, 32 . . . 20, 19, 18 . . . 4 3 2 1 . . . Kitty,' she said clearly.

Immediately one of the screens, a blue one as it happened, began to fizz gently and in a matter of seconds had resolved itself into a large moving (slightly blue-tinted) colour picture.

'Now we'll see what's happened to the girl,' cried the wizard-robot excitedly.

'Oh,' exclaimed Rosanna starting back with surprise, as she saw what the screen was showing.

'Is she being beaten or racked or otherwise tortured?' cried the wizard who was still bent double over the control panel.

'Not exactly,' said Rosanna hesitantly.

'Well, speak up girl.'

'Actually, she's not there at all.'

'What!' shrieked the wizard as he straightened up, his lights flashing at a furious rate.

'It's a bird,' said Rosanna, feeling thoroughly bewildered. 'It's a huge feathery bird sitting in a huge nest on the roof of a house which looks awfully like the one I live in, well the one I used to live in till this afternoon.'

The wizard came and stood beside Rosanna. He stared at the screen until his lights became dim with disappointment. 'He would be an odd bird if he wasn't feathery,' he said eventually. But the idea didn't seem to console him much.

'He is an odd bird anyway,' said Rosanna pointing at the screen. 'Apart from being so abnormally gigantic,' she could use long words too when she wanted, 'he seems to be talking on the telephone.'

'That's not very odd,' objected the wizard, perhaps thinking an argument might cheer him up. 'It's a perfectly sensible place to have a telephone. Much more sensible than inside a house. After all the telephone wires are right to hand. Makes for excellent reception.'

'But birds can't speak,' objected Rosanna.

'It was you who just told me he was speaking on the telephone.'

'I mean, ordinarily.'

'Oh, ordinarily,' said the wizard, in a bored voice. 'The real point is the bird isn't Kitty.'

'No.'

'You have let me down. DOWN!'

Rosanna jumped back nervously as the wizard suddenly turned on her and bellowed.

'Which means you weren't,' his voice sank to a reproachful hiss, 'concentrating.'

'Oh, I was,' said Rosanna, 'I certainly was.' Because after all she had been concentrating very hard on counting from forty-five backwards.

'Then you weren't concentrating on Kitty. You must have been concentrating on a bird.'

'Oh, no,' exclaimed Rosanna, 'not a bird.' The truth was that the only person that had slipped into her mind as she counted was her father because he could count backwards so quickly. And he wasn't a bird. Although . . . now that she came to think about it . . . she peered closely at the bluish screen again . . . that feathery creature on the telephone would have had a remarkable resemblance to her father if he didn't have all those feathers. Her father spent hours on the telephone.

Under the circumstances it might be most unwise to explain her lapse in concentration to the wizard. Could her father have turned into a bird?

'If at first you don't succeed, try, try and try again.' She was quite glad to have such disturbing thoughts interrupted by the wizard who seemed to have recovered his usual optimism. 'Wait for the magic word, press the switch and this time clear your mind of everything except poor little Kitty.'

'I'll try,' said Rosanna humbly.

'Kinhcet-rehcsif!' agreed the wizard in a positively subdued voice. The lights on his cloak were so dim that they hardly showed. The whole chamber seemed to have grown quieter and dimmer as if it realised that the finding of Kitty had become a very serious matter indeed.

'45, 44, 43 . . .' Rosanna suddenly found she could count backwards quite easily, '33, 32, 31 . . .' It meant she could concentrate entirely on the fate of poor kidnapped Kitty. '23, 22, 21 . . .' Tears started in her eyes and rolled slowly down her face. '13, 12, 11 . . .' Poor, poor Kitty. Where was she now? How was she suffering? '4, 3, 2 . . .' If only they could find her. 'Kitty!' she called out loud. Her voice rang out in a piteous wail.

The green screen shivered. The wizard worked the

controls frantically. It broke into lines, into triangles, into squares into waving lines. Then at last a picture. Both Rosanna and the wizard had their faces pressed nearly to the screen in their anxiety.

'Owwh! Owwh! Oowh! Leave me alone! You're hurting me! Oowhh! Oooh! Eeh! I want to go ho-o-o-me!'

They both leaped back and in their confusion bumped heads so that they sprawled onto the floor. The wizard recovered first. 'Eureka!' he screamed, jumping up and beating his machine-encased chest as if he was a gorilla. 'Sound as well as vision. What a triumph! What a genius! I'll be hailed as a new Einstein. I must write it up at once for the wizard-robot Scientific Investigator! I shall make my fortune!'

'Oh, poor darling Kitty,' said Rosanna trying to ignore what seemed a very unseemly display in the face of her cousin's (the girl looked quite like her cousin) terrible fate. It wasn't very easy to see her because the screen was suffused by a particularly poisonous shade of green but she could just make out a little girl's form in the grip of four or five horrible looking creatures.

'Are those the Washers?' she asked the wizard as he stopped congratulating himself for a moment.

'Those are the Washers alright. Ugly brutes.'

'Why is it all so green? Even their nasty mop-like hair looks green'

'It is green,' said the wizard huffily. 'There's nothing wrong with my colour balance, I can assure you.'

'Don't start all that boasting again,' said Rosanna who was really very concerned about Kitty. She had started screaming dreadfully again as one Washer approached her with a huge bottle of shampoo and another with an enormous very scratchy looking comb.

'Oowh! Eech! Owch! Go away! You've washed it six times already.'

'She'll have no hair left if they go on at that rate.'

'That's probably what they want. The Washers are terribly jealous of human hair because theirs is such a revolting green.'

'Why don't they dye it?'

'Because they're stupid.'

'No! Please! Help!' screamed Kitty. And Rosanna saw that a third Washer had approached with a sponge the size of a cushion. A particularly nasty thing about the Washers was that they didn't speak themselves but just

45

made ugly grunting sounds.

'Oh, where is she?' cried Rosanna.

'In a bathroom.'

'I can see that. But where is the bathroom?'

'Seeing as it's so green it's probably in Washer territory.'

'Oh dear. I'd be very frightened to confront the Washers. We once had a cousin helping who poked my ears till they bled.'

'The Washers are terrible cowards. All you need is a bit of really filthy, smelly mud and they'll run a mile.'

'I wish poor Kitty could hear us,' sighed Rosanna, 'and then we could tell her a rescue party was on the way.'

'Isn't it enough that I've established a brilliant audio-visuo communication link-situation to a far off country . . .'

'Is it very far off?' asked Rosanna ignoring the rest.

'Yes,' said the wizard, decisively. 'The flora and fauna sprouting between the Washers' toes indicate Nor, Nor West, compass point 30° by 26° .00085. We need transport.'

Before Rosanna could question or object the wizard had thrown various switches which not only wiped out poor Kitty but also plunged the invention chamber into total darkness. Luckily his own lights were winking merrily. For an instant Rosanna was amused by the thought that he looked very like the Christmas tree on the top of Selfridges, then she received a sharp prod in the back.

'Walk!' commanded the wizard who seemed determined to control the situation again. On the whole it was not much fun being an assistant, Rosanna decided.

46

'Where?'

'To the Queen. She has very good contacts in the transport world. It comes from having no legs herself.'

'What?' screamed Rosanna suddenly very frightened. 'No legs?'

'Surely you noticed,' said the wizard calmly. 'That's why she has all those draperies. It stands to reason. If she had legs she'd walk wouldn't she? Not lie around all the time.'

'How awful!' exclaimed Rosanna who didn't at all like the idea of that beautiful Queen stopping . . . well she didn't like to quite imagine where her lack of legs began.

'It's not awful at all,' said the wizard-robot. 'It's very useful. Doing no moving herself, she's had to establish a most efficient network of transport both short and long distance. Now do walk on up.'

Rosanna saw that a door had opened in the side of the invention chamber and that a steep flight of stairs began directly opposite.

As she started up them, she realised even in the darkness that something about them was familiar. Then as the robot's lights gleamed closer she saw the thick red carpet. These were the same stairs that she had climbed with Mary what seemed like weeks ago but must only be a few hours. She found it reassuring, though surprising, that she was going back up them in a perfectly normal way with the wizard. She would have expected an automatic jet-propelled tel-star comet rocket.

'Must get exercise on occasions,' said the wizard-robot as if reading her thoughts.

'Of course, of course,' agreed Rosanna, though she thought she detected a note of self-defence.

'Actually,' said the wizard as if her placating tone had reassured him, 'I don't want to shoot the queen up into the air again. And my self-propelled ejector rocket isn't absolutely reliable — directionally speaking.'

'I love walking,' said Rosanna firmly. She thought the wizard-robot could be quite sympathetic when he stopped showing off.

The Queen's bedroom door shone silver instead of gold in the night's darkness. Rosanna took a deep breath before she pushed it open. She quite expected further surprises. Even the wizard-robot looked a little subdued as if he didn't like the prospect of asking favours from the Queen.

However he spoke out bravely as they entered the room, 'Here we are again! Kitty located. Now it's only a matter of transport!'

ON THE EAGLE'S BACK

Rosanna looked round the room. The window was shut now and the darkness was lit by a multitude of candles. They poked out like pale fingers from gilded candlesticks on the tables, from curly candelabras fixed to the walls and from a huge but delicate chandelier hanging from the ceiling. The effect of so many glowing, quivering lights was to make the whole bedroom shimmer like a mirage. It wasn't a cold light, though, rather a warm, intimate exciting one, like when the curtains have been drawn before a birthday cake is carried in.

From the gramophone the swelling waves of several violins played romantically.

'Sorry,' said the Queen's matter of fact voice, 'I had my mouth full. So you've had some success?'

Before either Rosanna or the wizard could answer a huge deep voice broke in, 'Very late, isn't it? For you to be still up.'

Rosanna peered through the flickering candles and saw that a table spread with a white tablecloth had appeared at the Queen's bedside. And that seated on the other side of it, looking very at home, very large and very very frightening was the bird that she had last seen perched on a nest on the roof of her house.

'Oh dear,' she quavered, immediately assuming he was referring to her although he might have meant the wizard, 'I'm afraid I've quite lost track of the time. Is it after seven?'

'After seven!' thundered the bird, 'it's after eleven!'

'Is it really?' said the wizard-robot sounding interested and not at all frightened, 'then it's past my bedtime too.'

'Quite!' shouted the bird.

'Never mind, my eagle,' the Queen turned to him with a particularly soothing smile, 'the poor dears have been far too busy to think of bed. It won't hurt for once.'

'It won't hurt them but it will hurt me. Can I have no peace!'

'Have another glass of wine, dear. It goes so well with the Stilton.'

Rosanna watched amazed, as the eagle's feathers which had been quite ruffled up when he was shouting, lay back again into nice even layers and he poured himself a glass of wine. The glass of ruby red liquid looked most peculiar in his claw and when he lifted it to his beak Rosanna didn't know whether to laugh or be frightened by its sharp pointed end.

'This Corton-Charlemagne '69 is really very rich,' he said after a noisy suck, 'very rich and fruity.' His voice sounded quite mollified.

'Now my loves,' said the Queen who seemed in a delightful mood. She too was drinking the beautiful wine, Rosanna noticed, 'First you must have a bite to eat and then we'll sort out this matter of transport.'

Now that she mentioned it, Rosanna realised she was very hungry. She couldn't even guess how many hours had passed since her last meal.

'I'm ravenous,' she admitted moving forward, though keeping a wary eye on the eagle. Luckily he seemed totally concerned with alternate pecks at the cheese and dips into the wine.

'So am I!' cried the wizard-robot. That did surprise Rosanna who had assumed he ran on petrol or oil or water or a bit of all three like a car did. But on the contrary he joined her in a huge bowl of cereal which the Queen magicked up. It was as crisp and golden as the newest packet of cornflakes and sparkled with sugar like star-dust.

'That's better!' exclaimed the wizard-robot as they finished and the light on the top of his head became almost too bright for comfort.

'Good,' said the Queen, 'while you've been guzzling I've solved the problem of transport. Darling eagle!'

'Yes?' replied the bird leaning his feathery head forward attentively.

'You *will* fly the wizard and Rosanna to where the dreadful Washers are holding poor suffering Kitty.'

'Oh, yes!' cried the wizard.

'Oh, no,' whispered Rosanna.

'What?' roared the eagle, his black eyes flashing.

'Oh, darling. Do be an angel. After all, it is an emergency. Think of poor sweet Kitty.'

'I am not an angel! I'm a bird. If you want an angel, get an angel. They're two a penny in the sky at the moment. I'm a busy bird. I've had a very weary day in the nest. And now you suggest I start on a wild goose's chase . . .'

51

'Oh, no dear,' interrupted the Queen as serene as ever, 'if it was a wild goose's chase I'd have roped in a goose for the job. No, it's much too important for a silly old goose. It definitely needs an eagle, the King of the birds. Do fold your wings and have another glass of wine.'

'There's none left,' said the eagle grumpily. But he shut up his wings which had been flapping far too near a candlestick for Rosanna's peace of mind. She knew roast duck was supposed to be a speciality but she suspected roast eagle wouldn't be the same thing. Especially when he still had his feathers on *and* looked so like her father.

'You're such a wonderful King, too,' continued the Queen with her charming smile. 'You look after all your subjects as if they were princesses or princes.'

'Flattery will get you nowhere,' grunted the eagle but Rosanna noticed that his beady eyes were much less beady than before.

'Mary! Is that you!' the Queen suddenly bellowed. 'Not in bed yet?'

'The cherub woke me up,' said Mary, appearing from behind the door. 'She couldn't get her wings comfortable whichever way she lay.'

'That cherub would be much better sleeping with all the other cherubs on a nice soft cloud,' said the eagle rising from his chair and looking even more enormous than he had before. 'We might as well get this crazy expedition on the sky while the moon and the stars are still behaving themselves.'

'They keep going on strike,' whispered Mary at Rosanna's side. 'They're negotiating for a new top-rate since they're always on night shift. The evening star's being particularly difficult because he comes on so early.'

'I've never seen the stars look so bright,' said the wizard throwing up the window and craning his head out, 'it'll make it very easy to take bearings.'

'Hurry up! Hurry up!' cried the eagle hopping along to the window. 'Mat give Rosanna a hand and make sure she's got her safety belt securely fastened.'

'Safety belt!' exclaimed Rosanna in a surprised voice. But sure enough the back of the eagle was fitted out with all the advantages of the most luxurious car — and none of the disadvantages. It had soft downy seats but no whiff of the horrid leathery smell or the horrid petrol smell that made Rosanna so sick. The safety belts were made of a strong but light elastic silk that made her feel secure without cutting into her.

When the wizard-robot had climbed into a seat in front of her and obeyed an order to switch off his lights, 'We don't want to cause more union problems with the stars.' the huge wings slowly opened on either side of them.

The eagle jumped onto the window sill. 'Hold tight!'

'Goodbye, my brave popsies! Bring back Kitty safely!' called the Queen.

There was a rushing noise not unlike the noise of engines starting up in an aeroplane and then the wings were beating up and down and they were off.

'The candles!' wailed a voice behind, 'you've blown them all out.'

Rosanna swivelled round and saw that the bedroom, now fast disappearing behind them, was indeed in total blackness.

The only sound was the rushing wind and the wizard-robot's quiet but confident instructions to the eagle.

'Nor Nor East, Sou Sou West. Compass direction

.000823, keeping the Plough to your right and the Milky Way . . .'

Rosanna heard no more for her eyes had closed and she had fallen asleep.

She was awakened by a soft dampness dragging across her face.

'No! No!' she cried out still half asleep. 'Go away, you horrible Washers, I've cleaned my own face already.'

'It's not the Washers. It's a cloud. And it's time you stopped dreaming because you've been asleep for hours and we're about to hit a storm.'

The wizard-robot's unmistakable voice made Rosanna realise very quickly where she was. She sat up straight and looked around her. Instead of the beautiful black starlit night she had admired earlier, they were surrounded by an unpleasantly thick grey mist.

'A storm!' she questioned nervously.

'Yes,' said the wizard, 'the eagle didn't want to go below the clouds because then we'll lose the stars and get the rain but if it's really bad we may have to. It's a pity because another couple of hours and it'll be dawn and the end of navigational problems.'

At that moment there was a zig-zag flash of light that seemed to split the sky and certainly split the cloud, followed a second later by a roll of thunder — so loud that Rosanna felt it reverberate right through her head and down into her toes.

She tried to scream but as she opened her mouth the eagle suddenly stopped in his flight and dropped like a stone through the sky. Her scream was left hanging in the air above them. Rosanna thought that if it hadn't been for the safety belt she would be hanging up there with it. As it was she felt she would never be able to take another proper breath again. After what seemed like hours and when Rosanna was beginning to be quite worried about reaching the ground, the abrupt descent altered into a wide swoop and they resumed a horizontal course.

'Are you alright?' boomed the eagle's voice in front, 'didn't fancy being struck by lightning. Not when I saw the mood he was in. Really, it's high time the sky sorted out its industrial problems. They have more disputes than any other sector. Did you hear the thunder? You'd think he'd be keen on a peaceful settlement considering his age and position.'

'Is he very old?' asked Rosanna who had just got her voice back and thought it polite to show some interest in the eagle's conversation though she had no idea what he meant.

'Old? As old as time itself!'

'Talking of time,' interrupted the wizard-robot who didn't seem to suffer from Rosanna's need to be polite, 'isn't that something not unlike the first rays of dawn showing on the horizon?'

'Not already,' grumbled the eagle, 'the dawn chorus puts my nerves on edge horribly. There's a family of blackbirds who are all persistently flat on top C.'

Meanwhile Rosanna had been peering around unsuccessfully for dawn or horizon. She nudged the wizard's back, 'Where is the horizon?'

'Down there,' said the wizard looking over the eagle's side.

Rosanna looked down and only just managed to restrain her second scream in half an hour. There was the horizon indeed, a dark rim from which rose a pale grey light. But there also was earth. A dimly lit kaleidoscope of fields, woods, roads, telegraph posts and a few matchbox houses. While they had been flying up in the black night she had felt no sensation of speed apart from the rushing wind. It had been as if they were suspended in space. But now she could tell by the smallness of the trees and houses how high they were and by the speed with which they came and went how fast they were going, she felt absolutely terrified.

'I think I'm going to be sick,' she said to the wizard in a small voice.

'Oh, no! The eagle will be furious. Surely you can hold on. It's not much further.'

'I'm afraid not,' Rosanna could feel her face turning green and her stomach starting that dreaded rocking motion.

'No, I see not,' said the wizard hurriedly, 'Sir! Sir!' he shouted, 'We'll have to make a landing. Rosanna's about to be sick.'

'Quick, quick,' whispered Rosanna, hand across mouth.

'Prepare for emergency dive,' cried the eagle sizing up

the situation. 'Hang onto your hats.'

'Yippee!' shrieked the wizard as they went into the fastest, steepest dive possible. Strangely, the sight of the green land rushing towards them took Rosanna's mind off her problem so when they landed with a little bounce and a run she felt already considerably better.

'Oh, thank you, thank you. I am sorry. I'm afraid it was looking down that did it.'

'Always a mistake,' agreed the eagle in a surprisingly good-humoured voice. 'Never mind. It was time for a rest and breakfast.'

'Shall I get out the hamper,' cried the wizard enthusiastically.

'All in good time. Get out yourselves first and let's see where we are. The whole place might be teeming with Washers. We are in their territory, you know.'

Rosanna looked round nervously. They seemed to have landed in a small grassy clearing in the middle of a wood. The pearly morning light came in a funnel from the open sky above their heads and in low shafts between the trunks of the trees. It looked peaceful enough.

'It was very clever of you to find such a lovely green patch among all these trees,' she congratulated the eagle.

'Hmm,' said the eagle who was hopping about with his head on one side and his dark eyes flashing from side to side. 'A bit too green for my liking.'

KITTY IN DANGER

Rosanna looked about and saw as the light increased that not only was the grass green and the leaves on the trees but also the slender trunks and the undergrowth at their roots.

'Do you mean the Washers . . .?'

'Yes. Still, you've got to expect it in their territory. Doesn't necessarily mean they're any near at hand. Best thing is to eat breakfast and then be off sharpish.'

'Rightiho!' The wizard pulled a wicker basket from the eagle's back and in a minute had unpacked a huge delicious picnic. But sad to say, Rosanna found she didn't have much of an appetite. Nor she noticed, did the eagle.

'It's surprisingly clean round here,' he muttered worriedly putting down a cold sausage.

'Uhmm,' answered the wizard through a mouthful of boiled egg. 'A pity about that. No hope of collecting mud to sling at the Washers.'

'It's worse than a pity,' the eagle gave up all pretence of eating, 'it means the Washers visit the place regularly.'

'Oh, dear!' gulped Rosanna swallowing a piece of buttered roll with difficulty.

'And have you noticed something else,' the eagle stood up and flapped his wings, 'there's no dawn chorus.'

'That should please you anyway,' said the wizard licking his fingers greedily.

'No dawn chorus means no birds. The Washers can't stand birds because they make nests out of the sort of bits and pieces they consider dirty. When they find them, they spray a special detergent into the air that kills them after a few days.'

'Oh dear. Oh dear,' repeated Rosanna standing up beside the eagle. The light around them was so bright and green now that they all looked as sick as she had before.

'Quiet!' commanded the eagle. 'Listen!'

They kept quite still and to Rosanna's horror, the sound of many marching feet came clearly through the trees.

'Onto my back!' whispered the eagle. 'No time to clear the picnic.'

'Look!' whispered the wizard as he pushed Rosanna up and then scrambled after.

'Here they come!' cried the eagle as he began to flap his great wings in preparation to take-off.

Through the trees came a whole army of Washers marching two by two in strict formation. Their brilliant green mop-like hair bounced round their fierce pale faces. Their scrawny arms with the claw-like fingers swung backwards and forwards. The front three rows carried over their shoulders an assortment of long-handled brushes which had the sharpest wiriest bristles Rosanna had ever seen. At their head marched a hideously tall Washer who twirled from hand to hand a gigantic scratchy loofah on a thin rod. The second three rows carried brilliant green buckets which swung and jangled as they marched. At their head danced a particularly small Washer who carried a wicked looking pair of nail scissors. A third group carried alternately a giant toothbrush and a tube of toothpaste and they were preceded by another large Washer staggering under the weight of an emery board double his own size.

But then she stopped being able to see clearly because two things happened simultaneously. First the Washers saw what was ahead of them in the glade and at a command from their leader broke into a charge. Buckets banged and crashed, scissors snapped and the loathsome grunts that Rosanna remembered from the telepathic television screen issued from their mouths.

The second thing that happened was that the eagle roared into the air.

'Phew!' cried the wizard-robot. 'That was a near one!' Indeed it was for the nasty creature with the loofah had even got close enough to snatch a few of the eagle's tail feathers.

'Filthy beasts!' cried Rosanna. 'How Kitty must be suffering.'

'They think we're the filthy beasts!' shouted the eagle, with the triumphant tones of someone who had successfully evaded real danger. 'Just look how they're treating our picnic.'

Now that they were safely in the air, the eagle circled round so that they could see the massed Washers below. They were grouped round the remains of the picnic spraying it from long hoses with what smelt like disinfectant.

'I wish I'd finished that strawberry yoghourt,' said the wizard-robot regretfully.

'If you had it wouldn't be just food they'd be spraying with disinfectant.'

'You mean us?'

'Yes. And afterwards they roll the offending object in tinfoil and if it seems worth saving take it to the sluice rooms.'

'That must have been where we saw Kitty.'

'Quite probably. We were very lucky to escape. I guess we came down right next to a major military training ground. Those Washers were probably out on an exercise. They must have been new recruits or they'd have located us by the smell long before we saw them.'

'How terrible!' Rosanna shuddered. 'Do you think there's anything left of poor Kitty?'

'There's only one way to find out,' the eagle changed course and soared up into the sky.

'Not too far up. We're getting very close now and I want to try my new transistorised telepathic television,' called the wizard-robot whose lights had suddenly started flashing in a disconcerting way. From a panel in his left side he produced a pink and white striped television the size of his hand. As he pressed a button in its side an aerial unrolled and streamed out behind them like the tail of a kite.

'Do I concentrate on Kitty?' enquired Rosanna, trying to be helpful.

'Not necessary, this time,' said the wizard with a return to his previous inventor's brusqueness. 'Firstly I've already got the bearings and secondly we're very close. This is useful in two ways. One, I can tell by the focussing when we're exactly on target and, two, when it is correctly focussed we can see how Kitty's bearing up. OK. "kinhcet-rehcsif" and off we go!'

The wizard pulled a silver lever at the top of the screen and the screen immediately began to fizz and then changed into a picture of a nice pink and white little girl.

'Oh, how wonderful!' cried Rosanna with relief, 'she hardly looks changed at all. Just a lot cleaner.'

'And the picture's hardly blurred at all,' said the wizard proudly. 'That must mean we're very close.'

Both Rosanna and the wizard craned over the eagle's side and there directly below them was a long shiny green building.

'There's a wash-room now,' boomed the eagle, 'I'll start a descent.'

Soon they were close enough to the building to see that it was surrounded by high clothes-lines fluttering with clean washing and that every few yards there was a little square window. From one of these windows Rosanna could see something pink and waving.

Excitedly, she checked with the television screen. Just as she thought, Kitty was waving her little pink hand out of the window.

'There she is!' she cried, 'second window from the end. That's her hand.'

'So it is,' said the wizard also checking with the screen. But then the happiness went from his voice, 'the Washers are coming into her room.'

'Oh, no!' cried Rosanna watching horrified as Kitty cowered into a corner and three scrawny Washers approached with a flannel the size of a bedspread, a bowl of soapy water, the size of a bath, and worst of all one of the giant toothbrushes they had seen carried over the Washer soldier's shoulders.

'They probably left her to sleep in the night and now they're starting the morning session,' called the eagle. 'There's no time to waste.'

'But what are we going to do?' wailed Rosanna as the green shiny roof of the green shiny building grew bigger and bigger. 'How are we going to get her out?'

But if anyone had an answer they had no time to give it, for the eagle's claws hit the roof of the sluice room with a terrific thud and finding no grip went into a full-scale skid.

'Hold on tight,' shrieked the eagle, 'or there may be

more than Kitty who needs saving.'

'Water!' shrieked the wizard-robot.

Rosanna saw beneath them a deep mass of water that stretched round the sluice-room like a bubbling green moat.

'Washing-up water,' she gasped.

She listened to the sound of the eagle's feet scrabbling desperately to hold on to the gutter. 'I'm going!' he shouted. 'I can't hold on much longer!'

'Do you think it's cold?' whispered Rosanna.

'I can't possibly go into the water,' shrieked the wizard. 'My lights will fuse.'

'I thought you were a wizard!' cried the eagle. 'Here we go.'

'I'm a robot too!'

But his voice wavered because now they were over the edge and falling. Rosanna decided to hold her nose. She also shut her eyes again.

She therefore felt rather than saw the gigantic splash as the eagle hit the water. He hit it flat-bottomed sending fountains of spray up on either side. Rosanna waited for the water to close over head. She must remember to keep her mouth shut because she knew how revolting soapy water tasted.

She waited and waited. Then she heard the wizard cry out delightedly 'I couldn't have done better myself!'

Rosanna felt a gentle rocking motion start beneath her. It was like a — boat. She opened her eyes and saw that, sure enough, the eagle was floating on top of the bubbly water. He had folded back his wings neatly and his head, poised proudly high, looked like the prow of a ship.

'Well done!' cried Rosanna clapping her hands with

delight.

'Sshh,' said the wizard, 'do you want all the Washers in the world to know we're here.'

'Sorry.'

'The great thing is,' whispered the eagle though his whisper was equal to anyone else's bellow, 'that Washers can't swim.'

'How peculiar!' said Rosanna.

'Not at all,' said the wizard, 'it's like sailors. Water means work to them, not pleasure. You wouldn't swin in ink, would you?'

Rosanna was just beginning to argue that that was not at all the same thing when the eagle interrupted them sternly.

'They cross the moat by drawbridge. But as you can see it's pulled up now.'

And sure enough there ahead was a green drawbridge pulled up neatly against the wash-room.

'So that means the main body is away which means that the force we bumped into probably came from here. Which means we've arrived at the best possible moment to rescue Kitty.'

'But what about the Washers we saw inside?' asked Rosanna.

'They'll just be a small early morning cleaning force,' said the wizard. 'You could easily outwit them.'

'Me?'

'You,' repeated the wizard firmly. 'I can't possibly get my lights wet and the eagle must wait outside as the getaway vehicle. Anyway neither of us would get through the drainage pipe.'

'What?' exclaimed Rosanna.

'You do swim, don't you?'

'Of course I can swim. I won first prize for the breast stroke at the school gala.'

'Then whatever are you making such a fuss about?'

'But I didn't know. I mean the water's so green and soapy.'

'You'll have to hold your breath under water anyway. Now do you want Kitty to be torn apart by a toothbrush or not?'

'Oh no.'

'Good! If I were you I'd take off that silly dress while we're moving into position outside her cell.'

There seemed nothing else to be done. So, doing her best to look like Richard the Lion Heart (oh to be sitting reading a nice history book at school!) Rosanna undid her buttons and lifted her dress over her head. She was thankful now for her despised grey knickers which together with her white viyella vest made her feel quite reasonably covered.

In front of her she could hear the wizard giving instructions to the eagle, 'About three yards further along. That's right, hug the wall and we won't be visible to anyone from the window.' Rosanna realised that a little rushing movement she felt under her seat was the eagle's legs paddling them forward.

'I never knew eagles were amphibious,' she said out loud.

'Sshh,' said the wizard who seemed to be the only one allowed to speak. 'When we stop you must be ready to go immediately.'

'Where?' whispered Rosanna looking down into the deep water.

'To the drain. I told you.' The wizard sounded very impatient which Rosanna didn't think at all fair as he wasn't doing any of the dangerous work.

'Stop bullying her,' said the eagle who now he'd stopped paddling had time to enter the conversation. 'The first thing is to make contact with Kitty.'

'Oh yes!' agreed Rosanna moving back with relief from the edge of the feathery boat.

'My telepathic television won't work at such close quarters,' said the wizard sulkily.

'We don't need technology. Rosanna knows Kitty best. I just want you to call Kitty softly. The Washers are very deaf owing to cleaning their ears ten times a day.'

Rosanna looked up, saw the little square window, much too little for even the littlest girl to get through. She took a deep breath, 'Kitty! Kitty! Kitty! Kitty! Kitty!'

'You sound as if you're looking for a lost cat,' said the wizard grumpily.

'Try again,' the eagle encouraged her.

'Kitty! Kitty! It's Rosanna! Kitty! Kitty! It's . . . ' But before she could say her name for the second time, a pink hand appeared from the window. It waved frantically and then disappeared.

'It looks as if they're in there with her,' said the wizard who seemed determined on failure since Rosanna hadn't immediately jumped overboard at his command. He was silenced by a voice above their heads.

'Not at all,' it said shakily but joyfully, 'I'm quite alone. Oh I knew you would come to rescue me. I knew! I knew! I knew!'

'Of course,' cried Rosanna with equal joy.

'Humm,' said the eagle, 'we haven't got you out yet. Where are the Washers now?'

'I don't know. But not here.'

'Hhmm,' repeated the eagle, 'is there a grill in your floor?'

'Yes. Yes. A drain where the water runs away after all the terrible cleaning.'

'Good. I want you to remove it and wait. Rosanna will be coming in that way.'

'Oh, how brave!'

This made Rosanna feel much more encouraged than all the wizard's bossiness and she jumped up holding her nose.

'Quietly, quietly,' said the eagle. 'Mat, hand her the weapons.'

'Weapons?' asked Rosanna imagining heavy guns and and hand grenades like in the war films she wasn't allowed to see.

'Mud,' explained the eagle.

'Plenty of room for it in your knickers,' said the wizard handing her four smallish packages in waterproof wrapping. 'It's dry and light now but make sure it doesn't come into contact with water before you want to use it or it'll become much bigger and weigh a ton!'

Trying not to imagine this possibility, Rosanna stuffed the packages into her knickers. Once more she prepared to jump.

'Good luck!' called the eagle.

ESCAPE FROM THE WASHERS

Holding her nose and shutting her eyes, Rosanna jumped. Down, down, down. She felt her hair straightening above her. When her feet touched the soft bottom of the moat and she was desperately feeling for the drainage hole in the wall to her right, it was only as her fingers found the opening and she launched herself through it that she suddenly realised that Kitty couldn't swim, certainly not underwater anyway and that the eagle had suggested no other way of getting back.

But by that time it was too late to stop. Her ears were already popping and her one aim was to get out into the cell and the air before she burst.

'Oh, darling, darling, Rosanna!' Kitty's voice reached her throbbing ears. Then she had her face out into the open and with a heave her whole body. She flopped panting on the floor.

'You're a heroine! A real live heroine. Like Joan of Arc or, or Boadicea!'

'I thought of Richard the Lion Heart,' gasped Rosanna, 'but perhaps a woman would be more appropriate.'

The two girls sat on the floor half-laughing and half-crying until a voice from the other side of the window called out softly, 'Everything as planned?'

Then Rosanna recalled that although everything might be as planned she personally didn't know how she was to get Kitty out.

'Kitty can't swim underwater,' she called, trying to remember she was Joan of Arc.

'Then you'll have to use the main door,' said the eagle, calmly.

'Should be easy to open it from the inside,' contributed the wizard with what Rosanna considered misplaced optimism.

However clearly they had no choice. Besides at that moment, Kitty grasped her arm and hissed, 'The Washers. They're outside the door. They must have heard something.'

'The Washers!' whispered Rosanna as loudly as she dared to warn the eagle.

'The mud!' came the call back. 'Try and drive them to the drain.'

There was no time for further instructions for the door opened and two of the most revolting creatures in the world entered the room. Close to and in the flesh, their pale rod-like bodies and nauseating hair was much worse than Rosanna had imagined. Trickles of greenish water ran down their shiny limbs. They gave out a particularly nasty smell of disinfectant, toothpaste, and carbolic soap. They approached swiftly brandishing a length of hose and a pair of glinting nail clippers. Their thin mouths were open making their horrible grunts and they were so close that Rosanna could see they had no teeth left at all. Too much brushing, she thought, with some satisfaction.

There was no time to be lost. She pulled out one package and then another. She ripped off the plastic coating, rolled the mud in her wet hands and threw.

Thank heavens for rounders! The round blob hit the nearest Washer full in the face and, mixing with his watery coating, turned immediately into a thick black gluey mess.

'Hooray!' shrieked Kitty, totally confident in Rosanna's victory. 'Now for the next!'

'Wham!' The second ball of mud hit the second Washer bang in the face. Now there were two blinded, disgusted, terrified creatures staggering round the cell. The only problem was how to avoid their blundering progress and get out of the room.

Holding hands, the girls crept along the wall. As they reached the door they heard the most hideous grunting followed by a splash and a loud sucking noise. Turning round, they were just in time to see the second Washer disappear down the drainage hole. The first had already been sucked away.

'Hooray!' shrieked Kitty again, 'they'll be drownded dead! Drownded dead. Hooray! Hooray! Hooray!'

'Sshh,' reproved Rosanna, resisting the temptation to point out it was 'drowned' not 'drownded' — verbs were never Kitty's strong point. 'Do you want all the other Washers to hear?'

'Sorry.'

Still hand in hand they crept along a brilliant green passageway outside the cell. It was very narrow and reminded Rosanna of a tunnel cut in a hedge.

'Judging by the position of the drawbridge, the door should be near the end of this corridor,' she whispered to Kitty.

'You are clever!'

'It's very quiet,' Rosanna didn't know why but the silence frightened her more than a loud noise. It gave her no idea from which direction the Washers might pop up. But as they neared the end of a corridor a low swishing began.

'They're sweeping down the corridor towards us!' screamed Rosanna quite forgetting to be quiet and dragging Kitty behind her started to run down the corridor. As they turned the corner she saw in front of them the big doors through which they must escape.

Rosanna stopped abruptly. She took the two remaining packages out of her knickers and handed one to Kitty silently.

'Keep them at bay while I try and open the door!'
The door was bolted inside by a huge shiny rod.

'I can't! I'm too frightened. You haven't had a chance to look but I've lost at least three layers of skin.'

'It's lucky you've got twenty nine left then,' said Rosanna bracingly. She thought it was no time to let Kitty become self-pitying.

'And my teeth have lost half their enamel and my

72

hair is nearly as thin as a baby's.'

'Your mother always did say you were as bushy as a squirrel,' replied Rosanna deciding to ignore the teeth. Thin enamel didn't sound at all nice. Besides the sweeping was getting closer and was now accompanied by horrid grunting.

'Pull yourself together!'

Desperately Rosanna began to wriggle the rod along. Soon it was sliding out swiftly and then it fell with a great clatter to the ground.

'Quick!' cried Kitty, looking nervously down the corridor. 'Open the door.'

Rosanna turned the green door handle and in a moment they saw the bubbling green water and above it the bright blue sky.

'Escape! Escape!' rejoiced Kitty. Floating directly in line with them was the eagle.

The moment the wizard-robot had sighted them he began waving frantically.

'The Washers are coming back! Quick! We must take off at once!'

'Oh, no!' Rosanna peered nervously at the green land beyond the moat. Sure enough still in the distance but approaching swiftly was a whole column of soldier Washers.

Washers behind them and Washers in front of them! No time to lose. They jumped onto the eagle's back before he'd even reached them.

He began to flap his wings at once. Then he stopped. 'I'll never take off from the water,' he panted.

'We'll have to beat the Washers to the bank,' called the wizard. 'Paddle with your hands. That's it. One, two. One, two.'

Surprisingly, this worked well and they were at the bankside a good fifty yards ahead of the Washers. With some difficulty the eagle scrambled out of the water.

'Oh, oh!' gulped Kitty as she was thrown from side to side.

'Look!' cried Rosanna. 'The Washers inside have started to lower the drawbridge.'

'Take-off!' cried the wizard whose lights were blazing on and off in the way they always did when he was excited. 'Now! Take off!'

It was all very well him shouting 'Take off!' thought Rosanna as the eagle's wings flapped and rushed but he didn't have to do the taking off.

They all sat very still. 'I'm trying to be as light as possible,' whispered Kitty who had a very sweet nature but was not very sensible.

'Is there nothing we can throw out?' asked the wizard.

'No,' the eagle looked round. 'It's because I'm wet. It makes me heavy. And then with an extra person.'

The great wings were making a tremendous noise now but the most they lifted was a few inches off the ground.

'Oh, oh!' screamed Kitty. 'The Washers are nearly here. On both sides!'

'Oh, shut up!' cried the wizard-robot, perhaps forgivably under the circumstances.

'It's no good,' groaned the eagle, heaving and panting. 'I can't lift all of you.'

'Rightiho!' said the wizard, suddenly making up his mind. 'Rosanna and I will make our own way home. There's no point in putting everyone in danger.'

Before Rosanna could argue he had hopped out himself and she just had time to grab her dress before he'd dragged her after him. In a second the huge wings

74

which had never stopped beating lifted the eagle high in the air and Rosanna and the wizard were left alone. Water from the eagle's feathers dropped like rain on their heads.

Rosanna looked round. The drawbridge only had a few yards to go before it reached land and was positively teeming with vengeful Washers. The scene in front was even worse with a whole army of furious Washers only a few yards away. She could already hear their horrible grunts and smell their horrible smell. 'What are we going to do?' she said as bravely as possible.

'You are speaking to one of the most technologically advanced wizard-robots!' said the robot huffily.

'Oh, yes!' agreed Rosanna, trying not to look at the

oncoming Washers. 'Oh, good, I mean. Then you have a plan?'

'We might try jumping.'

'Jumping?' There was a crash behind them as the drawbridge hit the ground.

'Well, it worked before. We'd say the magic word, of course.' In front of them the leading Washer was bounding and snorting and spinning his terrible loofah.

'If you've got a better idea?'

'No! No! Let's jump! Quickly!' She could feel the wind from the loofah blowing her hair and hear the pounding feet of the Washers behind her.

'Rightiho!' 'Hold hands! Kinhcet-rehcsif!'

They jumped.

INTO THE LAND OF THE BOUNCERS

Down. Down. Down. Down. They fell for such a long time that Rosanna had to let her breath out. After a while she was even tempted to open her eyes which she had screwed tight shut, but then she decided it would be better to wait till they landed.

They did this with alarming suddenness, hitting something taut and smooth. They were immediately thrown up again as if it was a trampoline. Perhaps it was a trampoline. Rosanna opened her eyes.

'It's all black!' she cried as they came down again and then were thrown back up though this time only a few yards.

'You are difficult to please,' snorted the wizard letting go of her hand. 'I expect you'd rather be surrounded by Washers.'

'Oh, no,' puffed Rosanna who had fallen on her face without the wizard to hold on to.

'No thanks,' grumbled the wizard, preserving an elegantly upright position as he bounced in lower and lower bursts.

'Thank you, thank you!' This time Rosanna landed on her back which was, as a matter of fact, a definitely pleasurable sensation. If only it wasn't so dark.

'There we are,' said the wizard becoming steady and upright.

'Where are we?' puffed Rosanna who'd just made a final landing on her hands and knees. She sat up cross-legged.

'I don't know where we are but I know how we got here. I used my special Earth-crust-infra-red-telepathic-crack-detector to send us right through the Washers' world and out the other side.'

'The other side,' repeated Rosanna doubtfully, who couldn't help feeling that wherever they were it seemed more like the middle than the other side. 'You are very very clever,' she added after a moment's pause because it really wouldn't do to offend the wizard.

'I know,' agreed the wizard, 'a technological wonder boy. I have an I.Q. of 210. That's why I turned into a robot. Hang on while I turn on my lights then I might even be able to tell you where we are.'

This turned out to be an optimistic view. For although the lights showed up their surroundings very clearly it got them no nearer to knowing what was what. They were in a large black chamber with a black springy floor and that was that.

'Oh,' said Rosanna, disappointedly.

'I know what you mean,' agreed the wizard. 'Clearly we are not yet anywhere very much. What we must discover is a way out that is not the way we came in. You go round the wall to the left and I'll go to the right.'

Rosanna didn't like this very much as the further she

went from the wizard the darker it became. However quite soon they'd made a complete circle and met again. They looked at each other.

'Interesting,' commented the wizard.

Rosanna wanted to wail 'How do we get out?' but was afraid she might burst into tears.

'Feel like a bounce,' suggested the wizard after a pause.

'No thanks. I've done quite a lot of bouncing already.'

'Quite true. Mind if I have a little one. Might help me think.'

'Not at all.'

But she soon found she did mind. For every time the wizard landed she was thrown up into the air. Not very high. But high enough to be disconcerting. Besides she always landed so awkwardly. In the end it seemed more comfortable to jump gently to his time.

It was while she was doing this that she happened to look up.

'Oh, look, Mat, look!' Above their heads instead of the just one opening through which they'd fallen she could see whole groups of round black holes each one apparently leading upwards to some individual tunnel.

'Look where?' said the wizard who wore the blank concentrated expression of someone who was thinking of nothing but shooting up and shooting down.

'Look . . . ' But she got no further for just as the wizard set off on his upward journey a huge round red thing came whizzing down. Narrowly missing both Rosanna and the wizard, it hit the floor with an ear-splitting squeak and then shot up to the roof. Rosanna turned up her face just in time to see it disappear through one of the round holes.

'Whatever was that?' cried the wizard who had fallen flat on his back with surprise. Although rigid he still bounced slightly.

'It looked like a — a ball!' exclaimed Rosanna. 'A huge red ball.'

'A ball,' he repeated, 'a huge red ball.' He lay unmoving on his back. 'A ball. A bouncing ball. A coloured bouncing ball.'

'Yes. Yes.' said Rosanna impatiently. 'A ball. I was just trying to tell you about the round holes in the ceiling when it came whizzing down. It might have killed me!'

'I can see the holes now alright,' said the wizard thoughtfully.

'Well of course you can. You're lying on your back.'

'Quite right. This could be serious.'

'I told you I could have been killed, squashed flat. If it had bounced in on my head.'

'Quite. You'd be lying here as flat as I am now, except you wouldn't be able to get up.' The wizard suddenly knelt up. 'I'm afraid.' he said addressing Rosanna directly for the first time and looking very grim, 'we may have jumped out of the frying pan into the fire.'

'Oh,' said Rosanna nervously. It sounded horrid.

'In other words my crack in the Washer world surface has led us straight down to the world of the Bouncers.'

'The Bouncers!'

'Bouncing balls. Huge rubber balls of many hues.'

'Of many hues?'

'Colours.'

'Oh, yes.'

'Those round holes confirm it. At any moment

without any warning a yellow or blue or purple or purple with yellow spots or blue with red stripes or green with pink . . .'

'Yes! Yes!'

'May come right down and as you rightly say squash us both flat. You flatter than me because my electronic equipment makes me tougher but both of us quite flat enough.'

'How terrifying!' Rosanna looked upwards and tried to find a place which was as far away from a hole as possible. But there were too many too close together to make her feel at all safe. 'What can we do?'

'The bouncers are not evil, of course, like the Washers. They wouldn't want to hurt us. They might even feel quite sorry when they saw us squashed flat.'

'Oh,' shuddered Rosanna, 'I wish you wouldn't say that — about being squashed.'

'You said it first.'

'Yes. But you keep repeating it.'

'Do you want to know about the Bouncers or not?'

'Oh, please don't get huffy again. It's just that I'd much rather be doing something than talking.'

'Doing what?'

'Oh, dear,' Rosanna looked up at the ceiling.

'Exactly. We can't decide what to do till we've thoroughly examined their habits.'

'Well, do let's examine quickly.'

'The real point I was making is that the Bouncers don't want to hurt us. They'll just squash us . . . sorry . . . kill us accidentally.'

'I don't see . . .'

'Sshh. So if we can avoid them we'll be quite safe. Hey! Look out!'

Before Rosanna could do more than cover her head a hugh lime green ball with orange spots had shot past her left ear, hit the floor with the same hideous squeak and disappeared back up into the ceiling.

'Missed!' crowed the wizard. 'What we must do is obvious.'

'I'm afraid it's not obvious to me.'

'Jump.'

'Jump? Again?'

'Yes. But this time we jump like the bouncers do. One after another, aiming for a particular entrance to a particular tunnel. That's the way they get around. This room is probably used as a staging-post giving extra push for any Bouncers who are slowing down. What we've got to do is bounce into the system ourselves and then find a way out to another world — preferably not the Washers!'

'I'm ready,' cried Rosanna, feeling better now they had a plan of action. 'What about that hole? The big one to the left. I don't think my aim will be good enough for anything smaller.'

'Right,' agreed the wizard, 'prepare to launch! You go first and then I can give you a shove if you don't quite make it through.'

Rosanna fixed her eyes on the chosen hole and was just finishing a few preparatory bounces when a gigantic purple ball with something glinting gold on top came spinning towards her.

'Aah!' Just in time she dived sideways. She lay trembling and shuddering while the monstrous ball gave an almighty squeak before roaring upwards.

'I think you've just missed being squashed by the King Bouncer,' said the wizard and even he sounded shaken.

'I saw something gleaming.'

'His crown. Quick. Now's our moment. That big hole must be his special entrance. He won't use it again for a while. Are you ready?'

Rosanna stumbled to her feet and began bouncing weakly.

'Come on! Higher!'

'I'm trying.'

'Higher! Higher! If I had my jet-propelled-rocket-ejector machine we'd have none of this trouble.'

'But you haven't.'

'No. Spring!' Obeying his command, Rosanna stretched her body and tried to pretend she was a jet-propelled-rocket-ejector machine. To her surprise it worked and she found herself through the hole and on the edge of a black tunnel which rolled quite steeply down. The wizard landed beside her.

'So far so good.'

'I can hardly stop myself slipping.'

'Don't. The Bouncers roll. But we'd be better sliding. Pretend you're on a helter-skelter. Enjoy . . .' But Rosanna was already sliding down at a tremendous speed. It only ended when a hole suddenly appeared

below her and she felt herself falling through the air.
'Oh! Oh!'

'It's alright,' called the wizard close behind, 'just prepare to bounce.'

Sure enough her fall was stopped by another springy floor. But she had no time to notice more about the room than that it was painted in cheerful stripes before she bounced up again, through another hole and out into another sloping tunnel.

'We're certainly going somewhere,' cried the wizard. 'At the next room try to bounce higher and we'll see if we can move up a level or two. On the other hand we don't want to bounce right out till we're well past the Washer's world.'

'No!' gasped Rosanna who'd just seen another hole ahead. This time the walls of the room were blue and they crossed with a pretty yellow ball on its upwards path.

'Well done!' called the wizard as Rosanna, pushing off with all her might, felt herself soar into the air.

'What a wide tunnel!' exclaimed Rosanna as she broke out of the hole.

'Just as well,' replied the wizard. And indeed this tunnel was alive with balls all rolling along at a terrifying rate.

'Just as well it's one way too,' said Rosanna feeling quite dizzy as she was overtaken by streaks of orange and brown and mauve.

'Motorways usually are.'

The next hole was very big indeed and Rosanna found herself falling with a mass of other balls. The squeaks as they landed were quite deafening. She was very nervous about being hit on the way up, but oddly enough she arrived in a new smaller tunnel entirely on her own — except for the wizard, of course.

'Whatever happened to them all?' she panted, trying to slide a little slower.

'That was an intersection and service station. Didn't you see those holes in the walls? A lot of the balls bounced into them for a rest. We're on a side tunnel now.'

'I wouldn't mind a rest,' gasped Rosanna.

'Not long ago all you wanted was action.'

'After all, I'm not a ball. My school knickers must be quite worn out with all this sliding. They're awfully expensive, even if they are ugly.'

'Most little girls like sliding.'

'I'm not little and I prefer swings.' There was no time for further argument for another hole appeared and Rosanna was falling yet again. This time the room was decorated pink and pale blue and there were six or seven small Bouncers attended by two bigger navy blue ones.

'Bouncer nursery,' explained the wizard as they rose again.

'I see what you mean about them not being evil,' said Rosanna. She was sliding headfirst on her tummy for a change. 'It must be annoying to have us dropping in uninvited and bouncing all over the place but they never look the slightest bit angry.'

'Too stupid,' said the wizard. 'They'd only hurt us if they were told to. All they can do on their own is squeak and bounce and squash unwary soft visitors flat.'

'I'd quite forgotten about that,' sighed Rosanna, 'I suppose one can't go on being frightened forever. Besides I'm so tired.'

This was perfectly true for when they next met a

floor she only just managed to bounce up high enough to get back through a view hole.

'Not much further,' the wizard encouraged her.

'Couldn't I have just a little rest.'

'And risk being squ . . .'

'Alright. Alright. But I'm afraid my legs are feeling distinctly like over-cooked spaghetti. Personally I don't like spaghetti at all. But I particularly don't like over-cooked spaghetti . . . If anything I like it raw. But my mother says . . .'

'You're going to sleep!' An indignant shriek followed by a prod in the leg broke through her reverie.

'Sorry. I don't know why I started to think about spaghetti. Particularly when I don't like it. Mat likes it . . .'

'Rosanna!' There was another even sharper prod in her leg. But Rosanna was too sleepy to react.

'I wish I was flying in the eagle's back,' she mumbled. 'With Kitty. Kitty doesn't like spaghetti either unless there's an awful lot of tomato ketchup . . . But my mother . . .'

This time she was interrupted by another hole and if the wizard hadn't pushed her from behind she'd never have made it out of it.

'Flying, flying, flying . . .' she murmured as they started on a new tunnel. 'They might even be home by now . . .'

Meanwhile the wizard had started to pull various switches on his body accompanied by much angry mutterings, 'Girls! Silly sleepy things. No guts. No stamina. Still I can't leave her to the mercy of the Bouncers. Time we got out. Let's see.' He pulled more knobs and buttons. 'By my reckoning we've moved

Nor Nor East, 18 kilometers, followed by Nor East East, 19 kilometers, followed by Sou West Sou 23 kilometers, followed by . . . Yes. Yes. We should be beyond the Washers' territory by now.'

He leant forward and dug a pointed finger into Rosanna's back. 'We're going to ascend. You've got to make one final effort. At the next hole.'

'Fly, fly, fly,' mumbled Rosanna who was far too asleep to make out what the wizard was talking about.

'Drat the girl! Well, I'll just have to drag her up behind me. Shouldn't be impossible if my shoe booster engines work. They haven't for months, of course. But then that's all the more reason why they should today. After a good long rest. That looks like a hole coming up now . . . Of course there's no reason to believe that avoiding the Washers' world means we'll come up in our world.'

The wizard slid down a little faster till he was level with Rosanna. He gripped her hand tightly. Wouldn't do any harm to use the magic word under the circumstances.'

The hole, just wide enough for two, appeared beneath them.

'Kinhcet-rehcsif!' shouted the wizard with all the breath he had left over from jumping. But even so Rosanna didn't hear him. She was far too deeply asleep.

CRYING IN THE DESERT

Rosanna could feel the glare through her closed eye-lids. It felt as if someone was shining a very bright light in her face. It made her want to turn over and bury her head in whatever she was lying on. She wasn't awake enough to consider what that might be. Except that it felt agreeably soft. Perhaps she was lying in bed at home and her mother had just thrown back the curtains at the start of a lovely summer day.

This was such a nice idea that she opened her eyes.

'Oh!' She closed them again immediately. What a silly dream to think she might be in bed! Besides, her poor mother hadn't walked anywhere let alone into her bedroom for months. What she had seen was a white-hot ball of sun in a shimmering clear sky. The shape of the sun reminded her of the Bouncers. The Bouncers reminded her of the Washers. The Washers reminded her of Kitty and soon she remembered all her adventures.

She sat up gingerly — after all she might have broken a leg with all that bouncing. But apart from a slight headache caused by the sun, she felt perfectly well, if a little hungry.

She looked round. The first obvious fact was that there was no wizard-robot.

'Cooeee! Wizard-robot! Where are you? It's Rosanna! Where are you hiding?'

But she didn't say that again because the second obvious fact was that there was no place for anyone to hide. Particularly a black-cloaked wizard with a pointed hat and a mass of flashing coloured lights. In fact there was not only no wizard nearby but there was nothing or nobody else either.

In other words Rosanna was sitting quite alone in the middle of a soft sandy plain which was totally empty. The only thing to look at was the sun and that wasn't a very clever idea because coloured spots and wiggles began to dance in front of her eyes.

'Oh, dear,' began Rosanna out loud, and then stopped because she knew that talking to yourself was supposed to be the first signs of madness. On the other hand she felt as if she'd go mad if she didn't let out some of the thoughts that were spinning round her head.

'At least I'm not in the Washers' world,' she said, deciding to take the risk. 'There's not a speck of green anywhere. Nor a hole. So I'm not in the Bouncers' world either. That must be good news.'

Unfortunately even as she spoke these brave words she felt tears come into her eyes.

'It's just that I'm hungry,' she said out loud again. 'And I'm worried about the wizard. The best thing I can do is start walking. Action always makes one feel better.'

The only difficulty was to decide in which direction to walk since every way was exactly the same and the sun was directly overhead. On the other hand that meant it made no difference which way she started. So that made it easier.

'Off we go!' She stepped out smartly — which was not very easy as the sand was very soft and had an annoying tendency to pour over the sides of her sandals. After a few minutes walking her feet felt very hot and very heavy. The rest of her just felt very hot. She decided to have a rest.

'I suppose this is a desert,' she said after a moment. 'I used to think it would be very exciting to gallop across the desert on a camel. But of course I haven't got a camel. And it is so hot. And I am so thirsty.'

As tears threatened to rise again she tried to make herself laugh with the thought that they might be quite useful to quench her thirst. 'But that wouldn't work because they're salty.' she said out loud, 'which will merely make me thirstier than ever.' At which she broke into quite uncontrollable sobs and that was the end of conversation for a bit.

The tears, running down her cheeks and dripping off the end of her nose formed a small puddle between her crossed legs. And then a bigger one. Soon the most extraordinary thing began to happen. Because her eyes were squeezed tight with crying she did not see it. The first she knew about it was when something feathery began to brush against one of her legs. And then something prickly began to tickle the other. She opened her eyes which had become small and red and ugly and looked down.

'Carrots!' she exclaimed, 'gooseberries!' And as she jumped to her feet, 'Strawberries! Cucumber! And a huge fat melon!'

The most delicious looking lunch was growing under her very eyes. She had never seen such a tempting variety of fruit and vegetables — not even in her grandmother's garden and her grandmother was famous for her green fingers. Now that she was standing the puddle had spread further so that quite a large patch of what had been dry sand was covered with succulent delicacies.

'I never knew tears could be so useful,' said Rosanna, her mouth watering. 'Perhaps I could start a business in the desert. A market garden for Nomads. Or even a green-grocer. Except there aren't any Nomads in this desert. At any rate, I'd better start eating them straight away before the sun dries them up again.'

This was good advice to herself for now that she had stopped crying the plants had stopped growing and some of them were even beginning to crinkle at the edges. Since there were no grown-ups around to tell her otherwise, she decided to begin with what she liked most. It would be terribly disheartening if the strawberries shrivelled up while she ate the cucumber.

She had finished the strawberries and was concentrating on the melon which was sweet and golden and juicy when she realised a very odd thing had happened. She was no longer in the sun. Something or someone had come between her and its glaring rays. If she hadn't been so absorbed, with juice running down her chin almost as fast as tears had before, she would have looked up to see what was causing the shadow.

As it was she got the most dreadful shock when a voice which she recognised as the wizard's screamed in her ear, 'Grab my feet! Quick! Or I'll go off again!'

Before she could do anything at all a pair of black pointed shoes shot down from the sky, squashed the gooseberry bush flat and shot back up again.

'Fool! Idiot! Coward!' screamed the wizard, who was attached to the shoes, 'you've missed! I told you to be quick!'

'My gooseberries!' cried Rosanna. 'Ruined!'

'What does it matter about your gooseberries,' called the wizard whose voice was already getting fainter as he receded upwards. 'What about me? It'll be hours before I come down again.'

Rosanna stood up and shaded her hand against the sun which had reappeared from behind his body. 'Where are you going?'

'Up,' Rosanna strained her ears to hear his faraway

voice, 'my shoes. I turned on my Shoe Booster-Engines to help you escape the Bouncers and now I can't turn them off. It's all your fau-au-au-lt . . .'

He had become a small black spot not far from the sun. Then he had disappeared altogether.

'Oh, dear,' said Rosanna, licking her fingers guiltily, 'it does sound as if I'm to blame. And here I am stuffing myself with succulent delicacies while the poor wizard is bouncing up to heaven knows where.'

However this turned out not to be entirely true, for when she looked down she saw that the remaining fruit and vegetables had dried up to little brown bits of crackle. She wondered whether she felt guilty enough to cry again but decided that on the whole she did not. Besides there was always the chance that next time her tears might produce something nasty like stinging nettles or thistles.

Her clear duty was to prepare some way of capturing the wizard when he made his next descent. The trouble was that apart from the burnt vegetation she was still surrounded by the empty desert. Perhaps her best chance would be to pull off the disobedient shoes. Though whether she could manage both before he was zooming up again seemed very doubtful.

Rosanna flexed her fingers meditatively. Now if she had someone to help her . . .

'Oh! Not already!' She looked up anxiously for a shadow had crossed the sun. Sure enough, there was a black blob getting bigger as it fell towards earth. Trying to feel strong she crouched up with her hands outstretched. The sun was no longer hidden so she screwed up her eyes against its blinding rays and waited for the blob to turn into the wizard.

93

'Help! Oh! I'm falling! Oh! Help!'

Looking intently for the black pointed shoes, Rosanna was surprised by a voice that didn't sound at all like the wizard-robot's. It was girlish, high and piping, in fact most like her cousin Kitty's.

'Rosanna! Oh!' A small figure, a girl's small figure, tumbled down from the sky and hit the ground at a great speed. Huge sprays of soft sand went up either side. Rosanna found herself looking at Kitty – at least Kitty from the waist up. The lower half of her was buried in the sand.

'I thought you were the wizard,' said Rosanna stupidly.

'Oh no! I'm Kitty,' said Kitty with such a funny blinking look that Rosanna began to laugh.

'I can see you're Kitty now. At least, I can see you're half of Kitty. I hope the other half's alright?'

'Very well, thank you. Though rather warm.'

Rosanna began to laugh again.

'I am sorry. But you look so funny.'

Seeing Kitty's hurt expression she managed to contain herself. 'You see I was expecting the wizard. I was all ready to pull his wicked shoes off. And then you fell down instead. I must say I'm beginning to think this isn't a real desert at all. So many people drop in. Where did you come from?'

'The eagle's back, of course,' said Kitty. 'I don't want to be a nuisance but it would be most helpful if you could dig me out before my legs cook. It's really roasting down here.'

'How very selfish I've become,' said Rosanna starting immediately to dig round Kitty's waist with her hands. 'That's what comes of being on my own so long. I'll

94

have you out in a jiffy.'

'The trouble began,' explained Kitty who was trying to help free herself by wiggling around, 'when the eagle got involved in a dispute between the East and the West.'

'I think you'd better stop moving,' warned Rosanna, 'you're only sending the sand back from where I've just dug it.'

'Sorry. The East had been gradually moving left and the West was being pushed right.'

'Left or right depends on which way you're facing.'

'Oh, they knew that. Please dig harder.'

'I am trying,' puffed Rosanna who was digging as hard and fast as she could. 'But the sand's so soft. Of course, the real way to fix East and West is by the sun. The sun rises in the East and sinks in the West.'

'Where we were the sun stayed directly overhead. All the time.'

'Like here,' said Rosanna looking up and mopping her brow.

'I suppose it was here,' said Kitty whose arms and face had turned a bright pink, 'or above here. Otherwise I wouldn't have landed here when I jumped out. They attacked each other you see so the eagle said it was safer to jump out. Oh dear. I'm afraid my feet have definitely started to cook.'

Rosanna sat back on her heels and surveyed the visible portion of her cousin. She was afraid it had grown no bigger despite all her efforts. It might even have got smaller. Perhaps the desert was a quicksand. Better not suggest that to Kitty. She looked near enough to tears already.

Rosanna sat up abruptly. 'Cry!' she shouted.

'What?' Kitty stared at her amazed.

'Cry!' repeated Rosanna, excitedly. 'It's the only way I'll ever get you out.'

'But I can't.'

'Of course you can! I saw you gulping tears back only a moment ago.'

'I wasn't,' Kitty's face became even pinker with indignation. 'It was perspiration. From the heat. I never cry.'

'But you must!' shouted Rosanna who was sure she'd sunk another inch or two in the last few minutes. 'Think how roasting hot you are!'

'If I didn't cry when I jumped out of the eagle's back and hurtled like a stone to the ground why should I cry when I'm standing perfectly safe, if a little warm with my favourite cousin Rosanna? *You* cry if you want tears so much — as a matter of fact, you look nearer tears than me.'

'Can't you see,' screamed Rosanna, thoroughly exasperated, 'you're sinking!'

Kitty looked down at her body. There was not far to look now since the sand had nearly reached her shoulders. 'Oh!' she whispered, 'where have I gone?'

'And where are you going?' shouted Rosanna determined now that she'd gone so far to cause a whole flood of tears. 'Down to the fiery middle of the world.'

When Kitty cried, she really cried. One hiccough and she was off. Water rained down into the sand. 'Oh, oh, oh! I'm sinking! I'm going! I'm disappearing!'

'That's right,' said Rosanna approvingly, 'a few more seconds and we'll have you out. I've never seen such a deluge. I suppose it's because you so seldom cry, it's all saved up in a great reservoir.'

But Kitty's wails were beginning to change their tune.

Her eyes opened very wide with fright. The tears poised on the brim. 'There's something underneath me,' she whispered, 'something growing bigger. Growing bigger and pushing me up. I think, I think it's an . . . octopus!'

Rosanna couldn't help smiling as Kitty's voice rose in a terrified wail. 'No, it isn't,' she patted Kitty soothingly on the top of her head – which only reached her ankles, 'it's nothing to worry about at all. It might be a lovely strawberry bush or a tomato plant. I was going to warn you but I didn't want you to be disappointed if it didn't happen.'

'D-disappointed,' stuttered Kitty not looking very relieved, 'I assure you whatever it is it's much stronger than a little bush, it's pushing me right up through the sand.'

'Oh!' cried Rosanna beginning to be excited. 'It must be because you cried so hard. Perhaps it's a whole tree. Perhaps it'll push you right out into the open. I do believe you are rising. Yes! Yes! Here comes one arm. And here's another.'

'Oh, ah, ha!' Kitty began to giggle suddenly, 'it tickles. They tickle. I think you're right. Oh, ha, ha, he! It does feel just like leaves.'

'Here comes your waist!' cried Rosanna. 'And the top of your legs. I've never seen anything grow so fast. I told you crying was the answer.'

'I can nearly move!' exulted Kitty through her giggles, 'I'll try and walk out once my knees are free.'

'That's right. I'll take your hand and pull.'

But this turned out not to be as simple as it sounded. For the last part of Kitty's body came out with such a burst that Rosanna missed her hand. And in a moment in front of her horrified eyes Kitty was borne upwards on the top of a large bushy tree. Rosanna jumped desperately trying to grasp her leg before it disappeared out of reach.

'Quick! Lean over!' she cried. 'Or jump. Before it's too late.'

'I'm not jumping,' shouted Kitty who was clinging to a nice thick branch, 'or I might land up buried in the sand again.'

'You're not high enough!'

'Are you sure?'

'Oh dear.' Looking upwards Rosanna could not say she was sure. The tree had grown so fast that it was already nearly as high as a house.

'Oh, dear,' she repeated, 'why are people either too high or too low? Why can't they just be on level ground like me?'

She looked up again and saw with relief that a good portion of a trunk had now appeared so the tree couldn't be planning to go much higher.

'Actually, it's awfully nice up here,' Kitty's voice, surprisingly cheerful, carried down to her. 'There's plenty of shade and a nice cool breeze.'

'That's something, I suppose.'

'And now some lovely flowers have started growing.'

Sure enough within a few seconds the whole tree was covered with pale blossom.

'It's like fairyland,' called Kitty happily.

But in another few seconds the petals began to loosen and float downwards. To Rosanna, standing at the bottom of the trunk, it was like being caught in a soft sweet-smelling snowstorm. She tried to catch a few petals but they swirled out of her grasp and the moment they fell on the hot sand burnt up into little brown crisps.

'You'll never guess!' cried Kitty, 'what's happening now.'

'Yes I can,' shouted Rosanna peering up at the lowest branch which was still well out of her reach. 'That was cherry blossom. And now it's growing huge, crimson cherries.'

'Yes!' gulped Kitty sounding as if her mouth was already stuffed with the fruit. 'They're the most delicious cherries I've ever tasted.'

'That's all very well,' thought Rosanna sitting down in the shade under the tree. 'I don't begrudge her the cherries,' she looked up and then ducked as a hail of stones bounced down through the branches, 'even if it is rather frustrating for me to be able to see them but not eat them. After all, I did have strawberries earlier. But, on the other hand, delicious cherries or no, she can't stay there forever. I shall have to find some way to bring her down.'

She stared gloomily out into the gleaming, glinting, still empty desert.

THE MAGIC CHERRY TREE

'Oh! The wizard-robot!' Rosanna leapt to her feet. In all the excitement of Kitty's sudden arrival, she had quite forgotten about the wizard. Now high in the glaring blue sky she could see a black blob. A descending blob. Coming closer. Directly overhead.

Soon Rosanna could see the wizard's flashing lights, though they were pale in the sunshine, and his long pointed shoes. Suddenly Rosanna's expression turned to horror.

'Oh, Kitty!' she shrieked, 'mind your head!' The wizard was going to come down right in the middle of the cherry tree.

'What?' mumbled Kitty who was far too involved with eating to listen to any silly warnings.

'The wizard!' screamed Rosanna. Too late! His black flashing form crashed into the toppermost branches, stayed suspended for a moment by the astonished Kitty and then began to fall branch by branch through the tree.

'If only he'd get hooked,' thought Rosanna. But all

his equipment made him much heavier than Kitty and the smaller branches broke under him while he slipped by the bigger. However by the time he reached the ground beside Rosanna his progress was definitely much slowed.

'Oh, my bruises!' he groaned as Rosanna clutched at his shoes. 'I'm black all over.'

'You always are,' agreed Rosanna struggling with the knottiest shoe-laces she'd ever seen. 'Oh dear, you're going up again.'

'No! No!' pleaded the wizard, forgetting his bruises. 'Not again. I can't tell you how boring the sky is.'

But however hard Rosanna tried, the shoes wouldn't budge without untying the shoe-laces and the knots were unknottable — particularly as they reached eye level.

'I'm going,' wailed the wizard.

But then a remarkable thing happened. The wizard's black pointed hat now going at quite a speed came into contact with the largest lowest branch of the cherry-tree. It dug itself deep into the wood making all further progress upwards impossible. The wizard dangled under his hat like a puppet.

'Oh, dear, I do hope you've got a good chin-strap,' called Rosanna rushing to grab at his swinging feet.

'Take them off!' screamed the wizard.

'What *is* going on?' called Kitty, throwing down a handful of cherry stones. 'The whole tree's shaking. That is, the part that isn't broken. The cherries seem to be getting smaller too. Small and dry and shrivelled.'

'I'm trying!' Rosanna answered the wizard. She had no time for Kitty's complaints now. She'd make herself sick if she ate any more cherries anyway. 'I think one

101

lace is coming loose. Wiggle your foot around. Harder. There!'

With a clonk, the first shoe fell to the ground where it lay looking very innocent and very ordinary. Presumably its super booster mechanism only worked when it was linked up to the wizard.

'Now for the other!' The second shoe became loose almost immediately as if it wanted to join its pair.

'Done it!' shouted Rosanna triumphantly as she was presented with two bare dangling feet. 'Don't you wear socks?' she added as an afterthought.

'I'm not an ordinary person, you know,' said the wizard a little crossly though he added politely enough, 'but I am deeply indebted to you for taking off those badly-behaved shoes. It's a lesson not to turn on what you can't turn . . .'

But he was interrupted by a shout from above their heads. 'The tree! It's dying!'

'Oh, really,' began the wizard, 'as if we don't have more important things to think of.' But at that moment there was a loud cracking noise and the branch from which he was dangling broke in two and fell to the ground. Rosanna only just managed to jump back in time. 'Another opportunity for being squashed flat,' she said to herself.

The wizard lay on his back staring dazedly upwards. 'The cherries have all gone. The leaves are all withered,' he muttered to himself. 'I don't know how we failed to notice.'

'Help! Help! Help!' Kitty's distant cries began to sound more desperate.

'It's the heat!' called Rosanna. 'Nothing lasts long in this heat. I could have warned you.'

'My cloak,' said the wizard commandingly. 'That's how we'll save her. But you'll have to pull me out of the branch first.'

Spurred on by Kitty's cries, Rosanna soon had the wizard and his hat out of the wood. He immediately took off his cloak, and they held it out like a hammock below the shaking branch where Kitty was precariously perched.

'One. Two. Three. Jump!' shouted the wizard in his most commanding tones.

Why did everything to do with the wizard involve jumping, thought Rosanna.

'Go on! Kitty. Jump!' she called encouragingly.

'Ohhhh!' Kitty jumped.

Just in time. As she hurtled towards the outstretched cloak, the whole tree buckled and collapsed behind her. Branches, twigs and trunk crunched and snapped together ending up like a pile of fire-wood on the sand.

'Hold firm!' ordered the wizard.

'I'm trying,' puffed Rosanna.

'Caught!' They both shouted together. And there was Kitty neatly cradled in the cloak.

The happiness of all three lasted quite a long time. Then they gradually became aware again of the heat and the glare and the fact that they were still in the middle of an empty desert. They became very quiet. A few more minutes passed. Then the wizard-robot did a very odd thing. He knelt down and pressed his ear to the sand.

'Ha! Ha!' he said after listening intently for a few moments. 'My vibrator-sensitised-machine may have given us a chance of escape.'

'Do you mean your ears?' asked Kitty curiously as she and Rosanna joined him on the sand.

'No, silly.'

'I can hear something,' cried Rosanna excitedly, 'a sort of faraway rumbling. Whatever can it be?'

'If we're unlucky it could be the start of a volcano . . .'

'Oh!' gasped Kitty.

'On the other hand, if we're lucky,' continued the wizard imperturbably, 'it could be some form of transport.'

'As long as we don't have to jump,' murmured Rosanna under her breath. 'It does sound as if it's something moving along,' she said out loud. 'But very very faraway. I can't even tell the direction.'

'That's where my vibrator-sensitised-machine comes

in,' explained the wizard giving Kitty a smug look. He pulled out a small silver aerial from one of his sleeves and set it very carefully into the top of his pointed hat. It rose like a needle-thin spire swaying gently. 'This will lead us there.'

'Let's hope it isn't a volcano, then,' said Kitty.

'I suppose we'll have to walk,' sighed Rosanna thinking of how the sand had filled her sandals when she'd tried walking before.

But none of them had any choice. They trudged one after the other following wherever the wizard's quivering aerial led them. The sun remained high in the sky above them, the heat never diminished, the sand ran in and out of their shoes like egg-timers. But they trudged on and on. It could have been hours or days or weeks. Because nothing changed above them, below them, behind or in front, they had no way of telling how long they had been going. Only their legs moved more and more reluctantly.

'I never want to go to a sea-side again in my life,' said Kitty, shaking sand off her feet, 'I *hate* sand.'

'It's difficult to believe one ever thought it *fun*,' agreed Rosanna.

On they trudged. On and on and on. For hours or days or weeks. Rosanna and Kitty fell into a sort of exhausted trance so that they put one foot in front of the other without knowing they did it. Their eyes were cast down, avoiding the glaring rays of the sun.

'Oh!'

'Oh!'

Rosanna bumped into the wizard and Kitty bumped into Rosanna. The wizard had bent down to listen at the sand again.

105

'Ha! Ha!' he cried as he had before. 'As I thought. Very close now. Very close. I can feel the vibrations going through my whole body. I'll have to turn off the machine in a moment or I might become electrocuted. Let's try and pick up a bit of speed now.'

With the excitement of this news, the girls forced themselves to a brisk pace which they even managed to continue when it became clear that the desert had begun to slope quite steeply upwards.

'A hill,' announced the wizard, 'good. We'll be able to spy out whatever's making the noise from the top. We don't want to disappear into the middle of a volcano.'

'I feel hot enough to be in one now,' said Rosanna, mopping her forehead.

On they trudged. On and up.

'Fifty more yards,' called the wizard, removing the aerial from his hat. 'Thirty more. Twenty more.'

Making a tremendous effort the girls caught up with the wizard. 'Ten more. Nine, eight, seven, six, five, four, three, two, one . . .'

They were all in a line as they topped the hill and stared out at what lay below them so they all saw it at the same time.

'A railway line!' screamed Kitty. 'Oh, hooray! Hooray! Hooray!'

And there was. In the middle of the vast sweep of sand, ran a single line railway track. From their hill view it looked as small and fragile as a toy one. But its lines ran reassuringly from one side of the horizon to the other. It could take them out of the desert.

'A train!' exclaimed Rosanna sitting down abruptly as her tired legs suddenly folded under her. 'A train, was making that rumbling noise.'

'Quite,' agreed the wizard, 'I'd guessed that all along.'

'You might have told us.'

'I might, but I didn't,' said the wizard with irritating complacency. Although Rosanna suspected the reason he didn't tell them was because he didn't know. It was easy to be clever after the event.

'Now all we have to do is wait for a train,' she cried.

'There's no signal, I can see,' said the wizard, 'so we'll have to flag it down. Since we don't know how often they run, we'd better get down there as quickly as possible.'

'I can see it!' Rosanna peered downwards excitedly. A small moving line had just entered the left side of the railway track. Even from this distance they could see its bright red engine and yellow and blue carriages.

'Roll!' called Rosanna, tucking the skirt of her dress into her knickers. 'It's much the quickest way down.'

They rolled. Like three sausages. Or three logs of wood. Or three crayons. Over and over and over. Sand coated their faces and filled their ears and hair. But they took no notice. They could hear the approaching train quite easily now and all they wanted was to jump into one of those brightly painted carriages.

Kitty reached the bottom of the hill first. She was only a few yards ahead of the train's engine but she had the presence of mind to begin immediately shouting and waving her arms.

'Stop! Stop! Oh, please, stop!'

The engine had a tall funnel from which a column of white smoke lifted directly into the blue sky. Rosanna and the wizard arrived when it had already passed the

107

spot where Kitty stood, apparently without slowing its speed.

But, just as they were wondering whether to try and fling themselves aboard the moving footplate, there was a piercing whistle, a loud belch of extra smoke and a great shrieking of braking wheels.

'It's stopping!' shouted Rosanna. 'It's stopping!'

It didn't do this. That is, it didn't stop completely. But it did slow down almost to walking pace so that the wizard was able to turn the handle of a blue carriage door and throw it open. One after the other, they bundled through. And as soon as they were safely inside, a heap of arms and legs on the floor, the train picked up speed again and continued on its way.

Slowly, they untangled themselves and got up. The carriage was quite empty except for a bright orange bench against each wall. The wizard sat on one and the girls sat on the other. Cool wind rushed in from the windows on either side. There was no corridor.

They smiled at each other. They had successfully escaped the desert. Then Kitty opened her eyes with her little girl look and said, 'I wonder where we're going?'

No-one answered her.

FAT HENRY'S TRAIN

The train was going very fast now. It rocked Rosanna, the wizard and Kitty from side to side. The chug-chugging from the wheels was so noisy that it gave them a good excuse not to speak. Actually they were all far too busy wondering where they were going.

'At the moment,' thought Rosanna looking out of the window, 'we're still travelling through the horrible desert.' The glare from the yellow sand and blue sky hurt her eyes. She was just wishing there was a nice blind to pull down when her view was blocked abruptly.

'Tickets please!' said a loud voice.

They all stared in consternation.

'Tickets please! I can't wait here all day.' The voice belonged to a round pink face which was sticking through the window. It wore a smart blue cap with gold braiding. 'Besides I might fall off.'

'I suppose you're standing on the foot-plate?' asked the wizard recovering his voice first.

'None of your business. Tickets please. Unless you want to be thrown off the train.'

'Oh, no,' cried Rosanna anxiously, 'we've had quite enough of the desert for the time being. But I'm afraid the truth is . . .' she hesitated. She couldn't help feeling that she'd seen that round pink face somewhere before. It was a boy, she thought, about her age, even if he was being so bossy and official.

'Come on now. Have you or haven't you got tickets? This isn't a joy-ride you know.'

'We haven't got any money,' whispered Kitty sounding very scared.

'I'll have you know I'm a technological marvel,' blustered the wizard making his lights flash on and off at top speed.

'Technological marvels still need tickets.' The face was clearly not impressed.

'Henry!' screamed Rosanna suddenly bouncing up from her seat. 'It's fat Henry! The stupidest boy in my class at school. Whatever are you doing peering through the window of a train speeding through the desert?'

'I'm not fat. And I'm not stupid!' The pink face went red with indignation. 'And I've a great deal more right to be on my train, wherever it is, than you have. Tickets please.'

'You're not very tactful, are you?' whispered the wizard, pulling Rosanna back onto her seat.

'But it *is* Henry. No-one else has such silly round cheeks and silly round nose and silly round eyes . . .'

'He is awfully round,' agreed Kitty.

'Like a pig,' said Rosanna, thoroughly carried away. 'He snorts like a pig too because he always has a cold and never has a handkerchief . . .'

'Silence, you foolish girl!' interrupted the wizard. He stood up and addressed the face in soothing tones.

110

'Your name may be Henry and your school record may be less than impressive but anyone with a spark of discernment can see that you are a boy, no man, of power and influence.'

The face's colouring subsided to a more ordinary colour and his round eyes that had been rolling furiously like blue marbles steadied. 'Just in time,' he snapped, 'I was about to press the lever which controls the false floor to your compartment and have you all thrown out on the track below.'

'My friends here,' continued the wizard in the sort of charming tones Rosanna had never imagined she would hear from him, 'are suffering from sun-stroke and shock. They have no idea what they are saying. They are babbling like madmen.'

'Mad-women,' objected Kitty.

'You see what I mean,' the wizard waved his arm at the girls.

The face of fat Henry because there was no doubt it was fat Henry however powerful and influential, looked even more mollified. 'Well, if they're mad, I suppose that does make a difference.'

'Loony. Barking. Balmy. Crazy. Cracked. Batty. Mad as *haricots verts*!'

'What is *haricots verts*?' asked Rosanna.

'You see what I mean. Asking about a simple french vegetable when she claims to be top of her form.'

'Sad, very sad,' said fat Henry, smiling and shaking his head.

'How right you are. *Quelle tristesse*! As the French would say. And *tristest* of all for their parents to whom it is my duty now to transport them.'

'You mean you're taking them home,' said fat Henry

111

looking a bit bemused.

'That is my object. So that their parents can lock them in their bedrooms and feed them on bread and water till they become less loony, barking, balmy, etc.'

'That's not fair,' cried Kitty from behind his back.

'Sshh!' the wizard turned on her fiercely. He turned back to the face with his gracious look. 'So that you can see that they are not adverse to a further sojourn . . .'

'A what?' asked fat Henry with his bemused look.

'. . . staying in the desert. They might well prefer it to bread and water in a locked bedroom. But my duty is to take them home.'

'Oh, yes!' agreed fat Henry recovering his beaming smile, 'what a horrid time they have ahead of them!'

'Horrible!' the wizard shuddered, 'but then they are a pretty horrible pair of . . .'

'Loonies, balmies, crazies, crackers, bonkers, etc., etc.' supplied fat Henry happily.

'You are a quick learner,' complimented the wizard.

'Not really,' said fat Henry failing to look modest.

'So you can see,' continued the wizard, giving the girls a sudden huge wink, 'that all this talk of tickets has presented me with rather a problem.'

'Hum,' said the face trying to resume its official look but not quite succeeding. 'In other words you haven't got any.'

'That would be one way of putting it,' agreed the wizard.

'You're hoping, I suppose, for three complimentary tickets.'

'A'hem,' the wizard coughed apologetically.

'I'll have to ask the driver.'

'Oh?'

'But that shouldn't present any problems.'

'Ah!'

'Since I'm the driver as well as the ticket collector.

Rosanna, Kitty and the wizard looked at each other with alarm. In all the time since fat Henry's face had appeared at the window, the train had never lessened it rocketing pace. If he was the driver then . . .

'Who's driving the train?' shrieked Rosanna.

'You certainly are mad,' said fat Henry with a calm pitying look. 'It's on remote control of course.' He produced a round rubber ball attached to a flex. 'If I need to slow down I press this.'

'But don't you ever stop?' cried Kitty.

'Stop! Of course we don't stop. Not till we arrive, anyway. Stopping would be a terrible waste of time. Oh dear, oh dear! I can see the sooner we get you two on bread and water the better.'

'But what about stations!'

'And where are we going?'

'Mad. Mad. Mad!' laughed the round face, 'we're going *home* of course.' He turned to the wizard. 'Now if you'll excuse me I really must be getting along. I like to be back in the safety of the engine before we leave the desert. I hope you have as enjoyable a journey as possible in the company of these poor creatures.'

Tapping his pink forehead significantly, fat Henry removed his face from the window.

'Well,' said the wizard the moment he'd gone. 'You must admit I coped with that pretty brilliantly.'

'I can't say I like being thought mad,' said Rosanna sulkily. 'Particularly by a fat stupid boy like Henry.'

'So that's all the thanks I get for saving you from being crushed by the train's wheels.'

113

'Thank you,' said Kitty, showing her sweet nature, 'I don't mind being thought mad.'

'Fat Henry isn't in your class at school. You haven't suffered from his snorting.'

'What worries me,' continued Kitty, looking at the wizard as if she thought he knew all the answers, 'is why that Henry said he had to get back into the *safety* of the engine before we left the desert. Does that mean we're going through a dangerous country?'

'We'll soon know,' said the wizard looking out of the window. 'Have you noticed that for the last five minutes we've been going much slower?'

The wizard peered even further out of the window so that his head just about disappeared from view. 'We're climbing so steeply that if I didn't know we were in a train I'd say we were in a cable car. Technologically very interesting. There must be some sort of self-righting mechanism between the carriage floor and the seats.'

Rosanna went to the window. 'Oh! Help! Oh!' Below the window there was a sheer drop of several hundred feet.

'This is the outer edge of the track,' said the wizard. 'My side faces sheer rock. Much less worrying. We can change places, if you like.'

Rosanna's voice quavered nervously, 'If you don't mind I'll put the windows right up and sit in the middle of the bench with my eyes shut.'

'Vertigo can be a distressing business. Kitty?'

'I think I'll keep Rosanna company.'

The two girls sat pressed together, eyes shut. The wizard, hands behind his back, paraded backwards and forwards between the two windows.

'This is an interesting development. It appears we are

climbing by virtue of a series of Ss up a sheer mountain. One of the mountains, one may presume, we saw from the desert hilltop.'

'What will be at the top?' whispered Rosanna.

'Well, that is an easy question to answer,' the wizard chuckled to himself, 'the other side, of course.'

'I see.' Rosanna felt too weak to object that the top came before the other side. But the wizard as if guessing her objection, added,

'There're all kinds of tops. Some you pass without even noticing them. And others go on and on and on. Those are often indistinguishable from other sides. That's why it saves a lot of argument if you call them other sides from the beginning.'

'I see,' repeated Rosanna, still unconvinced.

'I'll tell you what,' the wizard went to the outer window, 'I'll put my head out and see if I can see whether we're nearing the top.'

'Oh, do be careful!' cried Rosanna, opening her eyes in alarm. 'I'd hate you to fall.' Now her eyes were open again she couldn't resist taking a quick look at the horrid space on one side and the cliff-face on the other. What she saw in the rock surface made her cry out in surprise.

'An eagle's nest! Just like the King eagle's on the top of our house. And there's another. And another. And that one has an eagle in it!'

Both the wizard and Kitty rushed to her side. 'Do you think that's our eagle?' asked Kitty breathlessly.

At that moment the light was blacked out from the window behind them on the sheer-drop side and a voice boomed out, 'I say, I suppose you couldn't spare a minute could you?'

Rosanna, wizard and Kitty spun round. A huge bird was spread-eagled against the side of the carriage.

'Sorry to interrupt and all that but I thought you might be able to give me a word of advice. Considering you're much the same species?'

As still no-one answered, the eagle became even more apologetic, 'I assure you it isn't my usual practice to barge into private parties but something has to be done. And as I mentioned, she is very nearly human — though not perhaps as well grown as you are. My name's Algernon, incidentally, but my friends call me Algie.'

'Oh, please don't worry,' cried Rosanna pulling herself together. He seemed far too humble an eagle to do them any harm. 'I'm Rosanna and this is Kitty and the wizard-robot. Of course, we'll assist you in any way we can. I do hope you won't fall off from there,' she couldn't help adding.

'I won't fall,' said Algernon, his round eyes blinking with obvious relief at her welcoming tone, 'and if the wind sweeps me off, I'll fly back. It won't take a moment.'

'So useful having wings,' commented Rosanna. 'For indeed if I asked you in I don't think you'd fit.'

'Wings is the problem if I may pick you up. You see the cherub will think she's an eagle. And it gets her into quite dangerous positions.'

'The cherub!' exclaimed Rosanna.

'To cut a long story short she's marooned on a cloud speared on the top of this mountain.'

'And you want to drop her into us.'

'Exactly.'

'Well. Of course. You're welcome. It's not our train anyway.'

116

'Thank you,' said Algernon beginning to flap his great wings against the window. 'I'll pluck her off the cloud and drop her when we reach the top.'

'Oh!' said the wizard with a disappointed look. He'd just started making his own plans for a Cloud-Pierce-and-Retrieve-System.

'I must fly now. It's been a pleasure to make the acquaintance of such educated minds. Once again my apologies for disturbing you.'

'Aurevoir!' cried Rosanna as he fluttered back from the window and swooped away above their heads. 'What a perfectly charming eagle.'

'Algernon!' mocked the wizard. 'What a silly name for an eagle.'

'I think it's very nice and old-fashioned like his manners.'

'Look,' called Kitty, 'I think we're at the top. At least we seem to be in the middle of a cloud.'

Indeed the carriage was filling with soft wisps of damp cloud, and outside the blue sky had completely disappeared. Rosanna shivered and wished she had a nice warm cardigan. The cherub must be frozen. Was that a faint sound of crying outside?

'She'll be here any minute,' said Kitty beating away a grey wisp that kept trying to wrap round her neck like a wet scarf.

But the next thing that happened was that they burst through the cloud and reached the peak of the mountain. There seemed to perch without any movement except a slight rocking. Perhaps it was just as well they didn't know that they were balanced on the very tip of the mountain or they might have been very frightened.

As it was the wizard said, with a smug smile for Rosanna, 'Looks as if dear Algernon has missed the boat. Now if I'd used my Cloud-Pierce-and-Retrieve-System . . .'

'I can hear his wings!' cried Kitty suddenly. She stuck her head as far out of the window as it would go. 'He's got her. She's screaming like mad. I must say, it is a terrifying drop. He's coming this way.'

'Well unblock the window, then,' said Rosanna trying not to admit how relieved she'd felt when the cherub seemed to have been left behind. Such a spoilt baby!

But at that moment the train gave a sudden huge lurch, forward, throwing them all onto the floor, and began to make a descent even more rapid than the King eagle's when he was avoiding the lightning.

As their downward path continued and grew smooth, the carriage gradually swung into an upright position and they were able to get up again.

'Well,' said the wizard in a shaken voice, 'that was a surprise.'

'It's like flying,' gasped Kitty.

'Er-humm!' said a voice at the window. And there stood Algie, his feathers blown back by the wind and an apologetic expression on his face. 'I'm afraid my plans didn't go as smoothly as I'd hoped.'

'They certainly didn't,' grunted the wizard.

'Owing to your sudden descent I was forced to make modifications . . .'

'What's that?' asked Kitty worriedly.

'In brief, I missed your carriage. However I managed to catch the last carriage. So I dropped her in there instead. It's just like this. Perfectly comfortable. You don't have to worry about her at all. Just deliver her back to the Queen on arrival. Now if you'll excuse me I really must fly. I'm wicket keeper in the Eagle Under Sixty-Fives B team and I won't be at all popular if I keep them waiting any longer.'

'But, Algie . . .' began Rosanna. Too late he'd gone.

'I do hope she'll be alright on her own,' she continued to herself, feeling rather guilty after her earlier mean thoughts.

'You should thank our planets we haven't got that spoilt brat in here,' said the wizard with no guilt at all.

'You know,' interrupted Kitty as the wizard and Rosanna looked like arguing, 'it isn't cold any more. In fact it's quite warm.'

The wizard looked up. 'We've slowed down,' he said, 'to our normal speed. We must be at the bottom of the mountain.'

'I think we're entering a sort of jungle,' said Rosanna doubtfully.

'Isn't it gorgeous!' Kitty stood on the bench behind her. 'There's creepers and swamps and monkeys and butterflies and parrots and gigantic flowers!' Forgetting all about the cherub, the three of them crowded round the window.

It was a particularly beautiful sight after the barrenness of the desert and the rocky mountain. They were travelling right through the middle of the greenest, most sweet-scented, flower-filled, bird-filled, song-filled jungle in the world. Creepers, decorated with brilliant pink tassel flowers trailed across the side of the train. Some of the flowers had as many as a dozen different coloured butterflies fluttering at their centre. Above them tall trees swayed and chattered with families of tiny long-tailed monkeys who ran along their branches or swung from tree to tree. Occasionally they glimpsed a clearing in which a pool of deep water shimmered temptingly. Often a pink stork or a blue-winged kingfisher stood on its edge as if ready to make a dive into its cool waters. Once they saw a splash and something brown and pointed disappeared into the water.

'It's like a dream,' said Rosanna, rubbing her eyes.

'Look out for the parrots!' cried the wizard as a stream of gold and red and green flashed cawing past the window.

'Oh, how I wish the train would stop!' sighed Kitty.

'Wouldn't it be lovely,' agreed Rosanna. 'We could swim in those beautiful pools and pick handfuls of those delicious smelling flowers and then try and catch a purple butterfly with orange spots.'

'A dream!' repeated Kitty.

'I think it's just as well the train never stops,' said the wizard. 'You girls seem to have gone soft in the head. It may look very pretty from here but who knows what snakes lurk under the leaves or what wild beasts in the undergrowth or crocodiles in the water.'

But although the wizard wore a serious expression the two girls were far too excited to listen.

Rosanna leant further and further out. 'Oh, Kitty, just look at that monkey. It turned a double somersault in mid-air.'

'Oh and that butterfly!' cried Kitty, 'I'm sure its wings have been dipped in silver.'

'And those flowers over there. So big and red and luscious. And those two great black spots in the middle almost like eyes. Oh, I wish they were near enough to pick.'

'There's some more this side much nearer,' cried Kitty, running to the other window. 'Oh, if only my arm was a little longer.'

'Mine is longer! Let me try!' Rosanna put her head out and her body as far as the waist. Her finger was only a few inches from the wide red petals. 'Give me a little lift, Kitty. Then I'm sure I'll reach . . .'

'Rosaaaanna!' The wizard whirled round as Kitty screamed with all her might.

FLOWERS WITH TEETH

Rosanna was alone in the middle of the jungle. The petals of the scarlet flower had snapped shut on her hand and pulled her clean through the train window. So far only one arm was captured but another flower was snapping at her foot and a third kept pulling her hair. She watched the train disappearing down the track despairingly. A little round face peering cheerfully out of the last carriage did not improve her spirits. What could one spoiled cherub do to help?

Now that she was surrounded by the sweet perfumes and the heavy greenery and the glittering butterflies and the chasing chattering monkeys all around her, they no longer seemed beautiful as they had before. It was all too close, overpowering, menacing. Even without the greedy red flowers flapping and snatching she would have been frightened.

The only way she could avoid them was dancing round in a circle, shaking one foot and then the other. She didn't dare try and pull out her trapped arm in case the teeth-like edges of the petals tore her skin.

122

When a large parrot with a yellow curved beak and luminous green wings brushed past her face, she let out a loud scream.

But the noise of the jungle was so great that it didn't even frighten away a single butterfly. Under the distinct sounds of birds and animals there was a continual high-pitched buzz as if the dark undergrowth of vines and twisted creepers was alive with millions of unseen insects. This sound, combined with the heavy scent from the flowers, gradually made Rosanna feel curiously sleepy. Her dancing steps became slower and she found it harder and harder to escape the petals' clutches. She even began to feel it didn't really matter if she was caught. She had seen again the two black eyes in one of the flowers and they looked at her with such calmness that she felt slipping down into them would be like diving into one of those cool ponds or into a lovely long sleep.

She was so very tired. Very very tired. How much easier it would be to stop fighting and let the flowers have her exhausted body. Her eyes closed.

A noise like the scream of a thousand cats burst into her ear drums. Her eyes opened wide. Instinctively her legs began dancing again. Just in time to avoid the biggest red flower closing over them.

'You are a naughty!' said a cheerful voice in her ear. 'Going to sleep like that. What would your mother say if you never came back?'

'Oh, cherub.' For the first time since the catastrophe Rosanna began to cry.

'Don't cry,' the chubby fingers tried to push back the tears into her eyes, 'or I might too and then my wings might get wet and then I can't fly half so well.'

'I'm sorry,' gulped Rosanna wondering how she could ever have disliked such a wonderful cherub, 'I'm just so pleased to see someone,' she sniffed hard. 'How ever did you make that terrible noise?'

'With my trumpet,' the cherub waved a long curled leaf in front of Rosanna's face, 'I made it myself,' she added proudly. 'It really put the jungle on its toes. It even gave those conceited man-eating flowers a fright.'

'Ugh,' said Rosanna starting to jump round more energetically, 'one of them nearly had me going in of my own accord. Those black spots must be hypnotic.'

'Oh, yes. They're up to all sorts of tricks. Does your arm hurt very much?'

'No. Funnily enough. It's just as if it's not there.'

'That doesn't sound too nice,' said the cherub whirring her wings, 'I'd better be off quickly.'

'Oh, please. Don't leave me!' Rosanna now looked on her as if she was her guardian angel.

'But I must,' the cherub looked surprised. 'I'm not strong enough to get you out. Actually there's only one person who is.'

'But what if those spots turn into eyes again and I get sleepy?'

'I'll leave you my trumpet. Blow it as loudly as I do every ten seconds. It'll keep you awake, scare the birds off and help me lead him back to you.'

'Who's he?' called Rosanna. But she got no answer for the round pink body with its bouncing gold curls had already flashed away.

The first Rosanna knew of anything unusual approaching was a tremendous agitation in the birds and animals around her. They had soon got used to the trumpet and were swooping uncomfortably close again. But suddenly they all began to move in one direction. Then the vines and creepers on the trees began to sway and soon the very tree tops were clashing one against the other.

Rosanna, although she had carefully avoided looking at the man-eating flower's hypnotic eyes, was exhausted now after all her hopping and dancing. She began to imagine the disturbance was caused by a tropical storm or a wild beast or even an earthquake. Perhaps a great crack would appear beneath her feet and she would disappear forever.

With her last ounce of energy she gave another blast on the trumpet.

As if at her command, the wall of green jungle shook

even more wildly and then parted. Swinging down towards her from the tallest tree came a huge brown man. He only wore a leather cloth round his waist and his hair flew behind him like a cloak. He would have been a frightening sight except that on his shoulder with a grin that spread from dimpled cheek to dimpled cheek was – the cherub.

'Wheeeee!' she cried excitedly, as the man let go of the thick vine he'd been swinging on and flew free for the last few yards, to where Rosanna stood.

'This beats wings anyday – at least my silly little pair. I must speak to the Queen about it.' Then seeing Rosanna's expression, who was staring at the man as if he was a ghost, she cried gaily, 'Rosanna, meet Nazrat, the strongest man in the jungle, probably the world. We wouldn't have been so long but he was halfway through his body-building exercises and I didn't like to interrupt him. They suffer terribly from cramp, these strong men.'

'Right enough,' agreed Nazrat, nodding his head. Under the mass of tangled hair he had a nice simple expression. 'Now, how can I help this little lady?'

'It's awfully kind of you,' began Rosanna but the cherub interrupted,

'Oh Nazrat loves helping people. He'd be terribly bored otherwise. I mean what's the point of being the strongest man in the world if you don't put your muscles to good use.'

Nazrat, who seemed totally under the cherub's control nodded agreeably, 'I take it, it's these here man-eating flowers that are causing the problem.'

'Yes,' agreed Rosanna nervously, 'you see, they have one arm   and . . .' but before she could finish her

126

sentence, there was a tremendous thrashing and screeching all around and instead of the menacing heads of red flowers there was a large patch of broken stalks. Even more astonishing her arm which she'd almost forgotten about, it had been gone so long, was restored to her body. Though it dangled a little limply as if lacking air, otherwise it seemed normal.

'Quite a bouquet,' said Nazrat.

He stood in front of Rosanna with a look of quiet satisfaction. In either hand he gripped bunches of the huge red flowers. He had to grip them tightly because although they had stopped the horrible screeching they were still gnashing their teeth and twisting and turning in a desperate effort to bite the iron fist that held them.

But as Rosanna watched, their writhings decreased and in a few minutes the red petals drooped and closed limply against each other. Then the red began to change to a dirty brown.

'Dead and ugly,' said Nazrat. 'In a moment I can throw them away.'

The wizard and Kitty had nearly given up hope of ever seeing Rosanna again. They didn't admit it to each other but each individually thought she had been away too long and they had travelled too far on for her to ever return. Both had noticed without saying anything that outside the window the character of the jungle was changing. There were no birds or animals or even flowers anymore and the greenery was much thinner. Only the tall trees remained unchanged looking more and more like leafy lamp-posts on a deserted road.

'If only we could stop the train!' said Kitty for the hundredth time. She got up from her seat. 'I'm going to have one last,' she corrected herself, 'another look.'

'Alright,' the wizard followed her over to the window without much enthusiasm. Kitty's hair blew across her face for a moment in the cooling wind and then straightened out as she stared out down the empty track.

'What's that?'

'Probably something in your eye.'

'No. It's moving. High up in the jungle. Where it's still quite thick.' Kitty didn't dare sound too hopeful. But she could definitely see something that seemed to be following the train's route. 'It seems to be gaining on us.'

'I see it now,' the wizard too tried not to sound excited. 'Something like a yoyo. It comes down from the top of one tree and then coils back up to another.'

'It's more swinging than coiling,' Kitty's voice began to rise. 'I do believe it's something swinging from tree to tree.'

'Or some-one!' cried the wizard. 'They could be using the creepers as ropes.'

'They are! They are!' screamed Kitty, 'I can see now.' Then her voice suddenly fell. 'At least it is. It's a huge brown thing with a long flowing black mane.'

'It's probably a gorilla,' said the wizard miserably.

'Yes,' agreed Kitty. 'Rosanna has short brown hair and a pale skin.'

'Their disappointment was so great that they both left the window and returned to their seats. They were therefore taken totally by surprise when the most horrible screeching noise was followed by a flying pink body followed by −

'Rosanna!' screamed the wizard and Kitty together.

'Wheeeee!' cried the cherub waving a strange looking trumpet over their heads. 'We've had the most glorious journey ever!' She whisked to the window and waved her chubby hand to someone they couldn't see, 'Thank you Nazrat, I think your muscles are spiffing.'

'Glad to be of service,' said a voice in the distance.

'Spiffing,' echoed Rosanna. She was sitting on the floor with a dazed expression on her face. Gradually her lips formed into a ear-splitting smile. 'I'm back,' she said, 'all of me.'

The nice thing about horrid things is that when they're over, everything seems so much nicer.

It was only when Kitty noticed Rosanna's face was turning a pale blue and Rosanna noticed the same thing about Kitty's face that they realised something distinctly worrying was happening. At the same time the wizard's lights stopped working. 'They're frozen,' he said in a surprised voice. 'Of course they are very sensitive to cold.' He looked at the girls hesitantly. The cherub crawled under his cloak.

Rosanna blew out a long breath. It hovered in a white streak in front of her. 'It is freezing,' she said.

All of a sudden both girls began shivering uncomfortably. They rushed to the windows.

'It's all w-w-white!' shivered Kitty.

'S-s-snow, I-i-i-ce,' said Rosanna through chattering teeth.

'It l-l-looks like the North Pole.'

In an effort to find some body warmth the two girls put their arms round each other and hugged close. 'Oh d-d-dear,' said Rosanna, 'and to think how I was complaining about the heat only a little while ago. Everything h-h-h-happens so suddenly on this journey.'

'I shouldn't put your head quite so far out just at the moment,' said a small voice from under the wizard's cloak. The cherub's warning was only just in time. As the wizard drew back a sudden smooth rush of icy wall only a yard from the side of the train enveloped them.

'A tunnel of ice,' whispered Rosanna.

'It's getting dark,' whispered Kitty.

'My hat's bent,' said the wizard in an aggrieved tone of voice.

'Luckily it's not your head,' yawned the cherub coming right out from under the cloak and stretching her wings.

It was very dark in the tunnel for after a few hundred yards no light could penetrate it. But just as they were becoming really scared and imagining white polar bears on either side, a faint yellow light began to show ahead.

They didn't like to be too optimistic but as it grew stronger it did look very like ordinary world daylight. Could the tunnel possibly come out in a land where there was neither blazing sun nor icy moon? They sat and waited as patiently as possible.

Their answer came quickly. Without any warning, like a cork from a bottle, the train popped out of the tunnel. And they were right in the middle of . . .

THE QUEEN'S BEDROOM BUT NO QUEEN

'The Queen's garden!' called the cherub and with a cheerful fluttering of wings disappeared out of the window.

It was the most beautiful English garden they had ever seen. A smooth green lawn was patterned with flowerbeds over-flowing with pink roses, white daisies, purple pansies and lacy-leafed wild strawberries. In the centre a little ornamental pool sparkled with a fountain spurting out from a dolphin's open mouth. Along one wall grew a few tall chestnut trees providing depths of cool green shade. Along another was a row of white and mauve and pink foxgloves almost as tall as small trees, along a third was a series of bright painted wooden huts halfway between green-houses and sentry-boxes. And along the last wall ran the railway track and their train.

'Please let it stop here,' prayed Rosanna. She had hardly finished speaking when there was a jolt and a scream of brakes followed by a loud voice which she rocognised as fat Henry's. It called over and over again as the train came to a steaming halt.

'All change! All change! All change! All change!'

'Oh, yes,' breathed Rosanna without taking her eyes off the lovely garden. 'I certainly will.'

But when she tried to turn the handle under the window to open the door it would not budge. She struggled for quite a while before realising there would be a door the other side too.

'Try that one, Kitty,' she said.

But when she turned round there was no Kitty to try it. Or wizard. Both had gone, as completely as the cherub had earlier. She was completely on her own in the carriage.

Still, this door was already open and beyond it in the wall which ran a few feet from the train, there was another door, a little green door. And that was open too. It seemed obvious where Kitty and the wizard had gone.

'But how rude,' thought Rosanna, 'after all the adventures we've been through together and after I saved them from the desert and Kitty from the Washers, how rude to leave me alone like this.'

She felt quite sorry for herself. But with fat Henry's 'All change' still ringing in her ears, she realised she'd better get out quickly in case the train got shunted into some dreary siding. Besides she had just noticed the little green door was slowly shutting and she wouldn't want to be caught on the wrong side of it.

'Wait! Wait!' she called which was pretty silly really since it was only a door. On the other hand it did seem to be shutting itself so it might be able to open itself too. Besides things round the Queen were never quite what they seemed. She thought of the flowers who posed themselves like ballet dancers in her bedroom and

132

the music that changed according to the mood and the light that turned from pink to white to blue without anyone touching a switch.

'I'm coming as quick as I can!' she called. And in a moment was quite surprised to find herself halfway up the stairs to the Queen's bedroom. Pushing the great door open at the top she cried gaily, 'I'm back!'

Her voice rang out but there was no answer. In fact, the room was empty. Worse than empty, deserted.

The Queen was not at home. There was no music, no flowers, no special light. The bed was there but the cobwebby coverlet filled with fluttering butterflies was replaced by a plain cream bedspread. The large window was there too but it was closed giving the room an airless, stuffy feeling. The dressing-table which before had been garlanded with necklaces made of shell and pearl was now bare save for one painted saucer. If it hadn't been for the shape of the room and the position of the furniture, Rosanna might have thought she had entered the wrong bedroom.

The Queen was not at home. Without her the room was nothing. Rosanna sat down on the end of the bed and put her head in her hands. She realised that during all her travels she had been kept going by the thought of the beautiful Queen waiting to receive her back and tell her how clever she'd been. And perhaps even let her snuggle into the cushions as the cherub had.

But now she was not only deserted by the cherub, the eagle, the wizard-robot and Kitty but the Queen too. It was very hard not to cry.

'Oh, there you are.' A voice at her knees made her blink rapidly. 'Tears at your age.'

'I'm not crying.'

133

'Not now.' Now she certainly was not because standing in front of her was the stocky little figure of Mary, the doll. 'But I am glad to see a friendly face. I thought the Queen never left her bed. I'm sure the wizard said she didn't have any legs?'

'The Queen's very pleased with you,' said Mary, not answering the question. 'She left a letter for you, propped up on the pillow. I'm surprised you didn't notice it.'

'Oh, where?' Rosanna scrambled across the bed and retrieved a large pink envelope from among the pillows. It smelled deliciously of roses spiced with lemon and 'Rosanna darling,' was written across in curly crimson letters.

Mary watched curiously as she tore it open.

'Darling clever girl.'

Rosanna read it aloud because she never found reading inside her head very satisfactory.

'I was pleased to hear about your rescuing Kitty and all your other bravery. The eagle was most impressed. What a pity I couldn't be here to greet you! But I'm afraid it was quite outside my control. Now be a good girl and get together all the members of the Right Side and come and find me on the top of Hampstead Hill. Past the Black Mud Pond. Through the Golden Door. And don't worry. Something tells me you can be a worrier. P.S. I shall expect you to know the second and third verses of "God Save Our Queen" when you arrive. P.P.S. Do take off those horrible knickers.'

'There must be something very wrong,' said Rosanna, frowning down at the letter. 'She wouldn't just go off. And what does she mean about "outside her control". Surely nothing is outside a Queen's control.'

'She told you not to worry.'

'But that makes me more worried. Why would she tell me not to worry if there's nothing to worry about. Perhaps the Washers have caught her, or the Bouncers or . . .'

'Hampstead Heath is terribly green,' interrupted a nervous voice just beside her. 'It could hide a whole army of Washers.'

For the first time Rosanna looked up from the letter and saw that standing in a row facing her were the wizard, Kitty (who had just spoken) Mary and Henry. 'We,' said the wizard solemnly, 'are founder members of the Right Side.'

'Do you know, then, about Hampstead Heath and the Black Mud Pond?'

'Of course,' said the wizard even more grandly, 'we are here to plan our campaign.'

'What we need is my train and lots of food,' began fat Henry. But was silenced by the wizard explaining he had just invented a new kind of portable cannon designed to fire lumps of mud at five second intervals. A full-scale war with the Washers was just what he needed to try it out.

'Oh dear,' said Rosanna, feeling herself going pale and noticing the same happening to Kitty, and even fat Henry.

'Don't worry,' cried the wizard, looking even more warlike, 'stuffed shirt Algernon eagle will be here any minute and the King eagle will come as soon as he has finished his run.'

'What?' said Rosanna in a surprised tone of voice.

'His run,' repeated the wizard nonchalently. 'Very good for the heart when the male of the species reach a certain age.'

'But eagles fly,' objected Kitty. 'They don't run.'

'He was wearing a striped singlet saying 48 beats per minute and had a pedometer strapped to his left ankle just above the claw. He had already done ten laps of the Palace garden and had five more to go.'

Then Algie made a dramatic entrance. He flew so fast through the open window that he hit the opposite wall head-on before he could stop. He fell half-stunned to the floor.

'So sorry. Brakes a bit rusty,' he mumbled in the humble tones that Rosanna found so appealing.

'Poor you,' Rosanna said sympathetically.

'Not at all,' Algie staggered to his feet, 'if I can perch here a minute and get my breath back.'

'Algernon come a cropper, has he?' bellowed a voice from the window and the King eagle came sweeping in. His presence made the room seem very small and everyone felt rather inadequate. They sat up straighter and put on determined faces.

Algie, looking as if he might have blushed were his face not covered with brown feathers, began to apologise again, 'So sorry, sir. Overshot the mark. Hope I haven't damaged the Queen's wall.'

'Self confidence, Algie. That's what you need, self confidence!'

'Yes, sir. Sorry sir.'

'Well, well! What's the plan?' boomed the King as no-one spoke up immediately.

'She's on Hampstead Hill past the Black Mud Pond. Through the Golden Door,' blurted out Rosanna hurriedly.

'I'll take you as far as the Heath. Can't spare time for

any further. I'm expecting an important call from California. Line up for boarding please.'

Rosanna, Kitty and Mary were carried by Algie, who though not too bright was very strong. And the King eagle, who was even stronger, took the cannon, the wizard and Henry.

Rosanna was prepared to enjoy the journey, although Algie's lack of safety belts made her feel a little insecure. 'So sorry,' he explained in his usual humble way, 'I've been meaning to fit them for ages but they're not compulsory for eagles yet so I'm afraid I've let things slide.'

Rosanna's real fear was that when they made their landing his braking system which had proved inadequate in the Queen's bedroom would prove totally useless with such a heavy cargo. She didn't at all fancy running into a tree or a wall. However she kept such thoughts to herself as she didn't want to frighten the others. They shrieked with pleasure at the views of London below them and Mary almost fell right out in her attempts to see the Tower of London. Eventually after miles and miles of houses and shops and churches (whose pointed spires gave Rosanna quite a turn each time they reared up — she wasn't too sure of Algie's steering mechanism either) they saw ahead of them a vast expanse of greenness. The King eagle put down smoothly between an avenue of tall oak trees. Rosanna shut her eyes.

'Wheeeeow!' shrieked Mary and Kitty, quite unconcerned.

Algie was going very fast. He was no longer flapping his wings but the force of his descent hardly diminished. Rosanna felt his feet unfold and hang down like the wheels of an aeroplane. They didn't seem to slow him down either. Oh for an ejector seat or even a workable parachute!

And then it was too late to worry. They were down. Down but not slowed down. Algie's legs worked faster than wheels as he ran across the grass. The girls were all silent now as they held on with all their might. Any minute Algie would lose control, a leg would give way, he would crash forward onto his head and then roll over and over, crushing his passengers.

Then ahead of them, Rosanna saw that the avenue was thinning and at the end of it there was a round brownish-black patch. She realised it was a pond. Presumably the Black Mud Pond. And Algie was heading straight for it. Using all his strength, he was still on his feet. But he could not last much longer. The pond grew closer. Algie grew weaker. Rosanna could actually feel his legs begin to collapse.

Then — whoosh! He had hurtled headfirst into the water. One by one, like peas from a pod, the girls popped from his back.

Rosanna found herself thrown over the eagle's head into the centre of the pond. As she took in a gulp of muddy water she thought that at least that proved the Washer's weren't around. Then she was kept busy splashing with her arms and legs to get to the surface. In fact this wasn't too difficult as the pond wasn't very deep. The problem was the soft mud at the bottom which seemed to be dragging her down and a mass of rushes and weeds which tangled round her legs and arms.

However once she'd got upright she found she was only waist deep in water and could wade quite easily as long as she didn't stop long enough to let herself sink. Anxiously, she looked round for the others.

The first sight she saw was the eagle, soaking wet and plastered with black mud, arriving at the edge of the pond with Kitty firmly grasped in his beak. That was a relief. Particularly as she was squeaking, 'Let me go. Let me go!' in a very undrowned sort of way.

The second sight was not so good. Only a yard or so in front of her Mary floated face down in the dirty water. Her beautiful hair spread out like yellow seaweed and her lacey dress dragged round her like a dishcloth. Rosanna hurried forward and picked her out. Her china blue eyes with their spiky black lashes were open but didn't look as if they saw. Water poured out of her well-shaped pink limbs. She felt very cold.

'Oh dear! Oh dear!' Rosanna shook her unhappily. But all that happened was that her eyelids clacked in a lifeless way and she had covered herself with more bits of mud and weed.

'Oh dear! Oh dear! She can't be dead.' Carrying her gently now, Rosanna reached the side of the pond and climbed out beside Algie and Kitty. She laid her on the grass in the sun. They all stared down at her dismally.

'Well, well! All present and correct then. Quite a dramatic landing, Algie. Lucky you found the pond, or there could have been some real damage done.'

It was the eagle, looking quite unruffled by events. Behind him the wizard and Henry arrived, puffed from dragging the cannon nearly the length of the avenue. Fat Henry collapsed onto the grass. The wizard gave Algie a look of scorn.

'What a dunce!'

Algie hung his head. His voice was muffled with shame, 'So sorry, so sorry, couldn't control, braking mechanism . . .'

He was interrupted by the King eagle who gave him such a hearty clap with his wing that he nearly collapsed again. 'Nonsense. Great show! Overloaded, that's all. Not your fault at all. Overload. Must be off now. Good luck!' And he had whirled away. They all looked sad for a moment.

Then a small voice made them turn round again, 'Where am I?'

It was Mary. She was sitting up on the grass looking astonishingly alive, indeed astonishingly normal. Since she had been lying in the hot sun, her clothes and hair were perfectly dry and since she had floated on the top of the water she was almost perfectly clean.

Rosanna and Kitty rushed to her smiling happily.

'I suppose,' said the wizard who always liked to know the *why* of things, 'once the water drained from your limbs you came alive again.'

'Quite,' agreed Mary, 'dolls get drowned for a bit, then recover once the water's dried off. I'd hate to be a human.'

'How about an eagle?' suggested Algie which

made everyone laugh.

Only the wizard didn't join in. He didn't find laughter very interesting — unless people were laughing at his jokes. He began to drag his cannon over to the pond. It was a very strange shaped cannon. At the front it was fairly normal but at the back it swelled into a huge bag-shaped lump. The wizard stationed himself near this bulge and all of a sudden a thick yellow snake uncoiled from under his feet and whizzed along the grass towards the pond. With a splash its pointed head dived into the muddy edges of the water.

Immediately the most nauseating sucking noises began and its body began to heave and writhe on the ground.

'You are watching one of the world's new technological inventions,' explained the wizard. 'An automatic mud-loading device.'

Henry who was more interested in this sort of thing than the girls went over to make a closer inspection. 'Ingenious!' he exclaimed admiringly. 'But how's it powered?'

The wizard looked even more proud than he had before (which wasn't easy). He tapped his chest. 'Me,' he said cheerfully, 'as you may have noticed I am the source of unlimited power.' He pressed a button just under his neck that set all his lights flashing so brightly that Henry jumped backwards. 'I can power my own complicated systems at the same time as loading the cannon.'

'Tremendous,' agreed Henry, 'but does that mean you have to stay attached to the cannon when it's firing?'

Not at all. I can switch it to remote control anytime

I please. Perhaps you would care to see the automatic mud-ball compositor device within the barrel of the cannon?'

'I certainly would.'

As the wizard and Henry bent excitedly over the cannon's internal workings the girls and Algie wandered past the pond and sat down on the grass. Mary opened a large packet of cheese sandwiches she had thoughtfully provided.

'I think we deserve a rest,' said Rosanna a little doubtfully. 'But not for too long.'

It was pleasant sitting on the soft grass in the warm afternoon sun. Soon they were all dry and the sandwiches were more than half finished.

'We must save some for Henry and the wizard,' said Rosanna in a sleepy voice.

'Yes,' mumbled Kitty, with eyes half-closed.

Behind them the noise of the sucking hose-pipe was reduced to a soothing glug-glug. The animated voices of the wizard and Henry became a distant meaningless chatter. Clearly it would be some time before they were ready to move or even ready to notice anything outside 'pressurised pump outlets' or 'button to control release gate for hand moulded mud . . .'

Kitty slumped sideways and her eyes closed completely. Algie put his head under his wing and began to snore gently. Mary's doll eyes snapped shut. At last only Rosanna was left awake. She looked round at the others unhappily. She knew she shouldn't have let them go to sleep. What if something happened? Anyone could creep up on them unawares. The wizard and Henry were far too busy to notice. At very least she must stay awake herself to act as guard. But her eyelids felt as if something was pressing them down and the smell of the cut grass was so sweet and the glug-glug of the hose almost like a lullaby . . .

Rosanna lay face down and fell into a deep sleep.

If the female (and ornothological) members of 'The Right Side' hadn't been so keen to rest they might have noticed something about the patch of grass they had chosen for their picnic. For it was a much cleaner and brighter green than the grass near the pond or indeed the grass between the avenue leading up to the pond. In fact there was a quite noticeable line about a hundred yards beyond the pond where the colour changed. It was almost as if someone or something had cleaned the grass up to a certain point and then stopped.

The sun was beginning to sink now. Very slowly. But strangely enough the light did not seem to become more golden as it usually does in the late afternoons. On the contrary the sleeping faces were becoming tinged by a palish green. The trunks of the trees beyond where they lay were also more green than brown. They grew thickly, sometimes almost touching each other, making a screen for what lay behind. They had been almost unmoving, only rustling occasionally with a bird in their leaves or giving a little creak as a breeze bent their branches. But now suddenly there was movement round their trunks. Shadowy, silent movement. Now and again something twig-like topped with a brilliant green, appeared for a moment before flitting behind the next tree. All the time they were coming closer to the sleeping figures. In the distance the wizard continued his lecture to Henry.

'You see,' he said, 'when I press this button the gate lifts, allowing the hardened mud now shaped like a ball — to fall into the chamber . . .'

'And the actual firing? How does it fire?' Henry bent even closer over the cannon.

Neither of them saw a circle of rod-like creatures with green mopheads close round the rest of The Right Side.

'I can't breathe,' gasped Rosanna.

'It's the disinfectant,' said Kitty knowingly. 'It makes your eyes sting dreadfully,' she added, trying to get to her hands and knees. But every time they rose even a few inches from the ground a new jet came to knock them flat again. Finally they lay still, out of breath, defeated.

Now they could see just how many Washers had attacked them. They were completely surrounded by an army that stretched so far back into the trees that they couldn't even see where it ended. The six Washers who had jumped on them were merely an advance party supported by the hose regiment and all the ranks of infantry.

'There's absolutely nothing we can do,' said Rosanna, pushing her dripping hair out of her eyes. 'There're far too many of them.'

Her words were interrupted by a rush and whir of wings as Algie at last broke loose and burst into the air. It was difficult for him to fly because his wings were wet with disinfectant but he was strong and determined. If he could only dodge the arcs of water which the Washers fired at him like tracer bullets.

'Go on, Algie! You can do it!' cried Rosanna encouragingly but she quickly subsided as a jet of water shot straight into her mouth.

'And then he'll alert the wizard and fat Henry,' whispered Kitty, saying what was in all their minds. But there was not much time to contemplate this happy prospect for at that moment Algie fell from the sky in a sodden heap. He almost crushed poor Kitty.

'I'm sorry, I'm so very sorry, Oh dear I'm sorry,' he began in his usual humble way.

'I'm no good for anything. That's the truth. In fact I probably do more harm than good.' A large tear escaped from his beady bird eye and rolled down his wet feathered cheek.

'Oh don't say that, dear Algie,' implored Kitty who had recovered from her crushing and had a very soft heart. 'Look at how you flew us all here.'

'And dumped you in the black mud pond.' Another tear popped out from the other eye.

'Oh do cheer up,' pleaded Kitty looking ready to cry herself.

'Be a man!' cried Rosanna, exasperated. She could see the first three ranks of Washers marching in towards them.

'He can't. He's an eagle,' said Mary in a matter of fact tone that would have made them laugh in any other circumstances.

The Washers were now only a few yards away. Rosanna remembered when they had been only a few yards from capturing her. On that occasion the wizard had said the magic word which had projected them into the land of the Bouncers and started the whole train of adventures eventually resulting in their safe return home. Now there was no wizard. Why, oh why, did boys become blind, and deaf, when they were studying a mechanical object?

'I suppose we'd better wave a white flag,' she said unhappily. 'Anybody got a handkerchief?'

Nobody had. 'My knickers are white,' suggested Kitty. But on examination they turned out to be the colour of the dirty pond. Definitely not white.

'We'd better put up our hands then,' said Rosanna.

'I haven't got a hand,' said Algie in a very small voice.

'I'm sorry. I really am a total failure.'

'You've got a claw, haven't you?'

'Oh yes. Two.'

'Put them up, then.'

But this proved easier said than done because if Algie put up both claws he fell flat on his face.

So the Washers, closing in for the capture, found themselves confronted by two little girls and one doll with their hands in the air and one eagle lying on his back with his claws in the air. It was a very peculiar sight.

Meanwhile back at the pond-side, the wizard and Henry were just beginning to be ready to think about something other than their cannon. This was partly because the wizard had explained every remarkable aspect of its design at least six times so there was really nothing more to remark or discuss. And partly because for the last quarter of an hour fat Henry had been complaining of an empty hole in his stomach.

'It's very bad for you, you know, to go without food for too long. If the sugar content falls below a certain level in your blood it hasn't the energy to reach up to your brain and quite soon you become paralysed with hunger. My mother knows about these sort of things. She never lets me go anywhere without a bag of sweets.'

Eventually the wizard was worn down. 'Mary was carrying the sort of basket that's packed full with fat sandwiches,' he admitted.

'Let's go after them at once!' cried Henry greedily, adding with a touch of pathos, 'before we're too weak to move.'

So the wizard and Henry set off in the direction the girls had taken. They, unlike the girls, soon noticed the increasing greenness of the grass and trees around them.

'I don't like it,' the wizard stopped, worriedly.

'I'm so hungry!' wailed Henry. 'My legs are shaking. Let's get on!'

The wizard allowed himself to be persuaded but insisted they proceeded cautiously without talking. It was lucky they did. Because all of a sudden they found their way blocked by a solid line of Washers. Their backs turned towards them. It was the last row of the Washer army which surrounded the girls.

The wizard came to a halt so suddenly that Henry ran into him.

'Sshhh!' He turned off his lights and pointed back the way they'd come. Henry looked miserable and tightened his belt by a hole. But even he realised they couldn't fight through an army of Washers for a packet of sandwiches.

When they'd retreated out of ear-shot, they both began talking at once.

'I wonder how long they've been there?'

'They must have captured the girls.'

'They obviously won't come this way. Too afraid of the dirt.'

'We must wheel up the cannon immediately.'

'And attack while surprise is on our side.'

'Before it's too late for the girls.'

'And Algie.'

'And the sandwiches.'

In full agreement, they ran the rest of the way back to the pond. The sight of the cannon immediately made their hopes rise. It looked so solid and efficient.

'It's heavy,' said the wizard. 'We must pull together.'

Henry eyed the cannon nervously, 'my legs are much too weak to move that huge thing.'

'Well, you've got to,' said the wizard firmly.

Pushing and pulling with all their might, it took about ten minutes to bring them once more in sight of the Washers' backs. They had moved slightly further away as if they were tightening the circle on their captives.

'We should still be in time,' said the wizard confidently, 'they always spend a long time disinfecting their enemies before removing them.'

'They can't have removed them because they're still there,' said Henry who (as later events were to prove) although fat, was not always stupid.

'I wonder how disinfected sandwiches taste,' retaliated the wizard meanly.

They wheeled the cannon carefully forward so that they had the maximum number of Washers in their sights.

'Oh dear,' said Henry, 'after we've got the first lot, won't they just turn on us and overwhelm us.'

'You've got to remember,' said the wizard seriously, 'that they're absolutely *TERRIFIED* of mud.'

He stationed himself behind the cannon and turned on his power system. Obediently the bag at the back of the cannon began to quiver. 'Remember if you're approached by an individual Washer, pick up a bit of dirt and throw! We'll fire on Go! He paused and took a deep breath. Henry looked at him expectantly.

'Are you ready? Are you steady? GO!'

The cannon vibrated and then lifted slightly. For a terrible moment it seemed as if one of the gate mechanisms had stuck, blocking the mud ball's exit. Then with a great explosion the first ball of rock-hard mud shot out, quickly followed by another and another and another.

'Dead on target!' screamed Henry jumping up and down (his legs seemed to have suddenly strengthened).

'Got one! Got two! Got three, four, five!' shouted the wizard as the balls thundered into the Washers knocking them down like nine-pins.

'They've seen it's mud! They've seen it's mud!' cried Henry. They watched joyfully as the unhurt Washers bent to examine what had knocked over their colleagues and then leapt away, in horror.

'Ugh! Ugh! Ugh!' They could hear their terrified grunts.

'In a moment, they'll be a stampede,' yelled the wizard. 'Away from us.'

'Yaa! Boo! Sucks! To the Washers!' Henry's round face looked as if it might pop with excitement. The wizard smiled indulgently.

The first indication to the girls and Algie that something unexpected was happening was a jostling and pushing among the rows of Washers encircling them. It was taking place to their left in the direction of the pond. The jostling seemed to be caused by the back rows trying to push through the front rows. Since they wouldn't move it was merely resulting in grunting and confusion.

The girls couldn't see very well because although the Washers were no longer firing the strong jets of disinfectant water at them, they were still being washed over by a constant light spray. As yet the Washers had not returned with the brushes but they knew it was only a matter of time. A column of Washers armed with brushes, loofahs, flannels, sponges, emery boards and other horrible armaments, were lined up waiting for the command to attack.

'You don't think that rumpus could have anything to do with the boys, do you?' muttered Rosanna. She muttered because if she opened her mouth more than a crack it was filled with disinfectant.

At that moment the front two lines to their left broke and the Washers (fleeing as we know from the cannon balls) burst out into the grassy patch where the girls were held. Instinctively the Washers wielding the hoses turned them onto the area of noise and confusion.

Naturally since there was no enemy, for the cannon

and the boys were too far away, they only caused more confusion among their own demoralised army.

'This could be our moment to escape,' muttered Rosanna. And then realising the hoses were not directed towards them anymore, shouted, 'Let's run!'

'Wait!' Algie looked round anxiously. 'We're still surrounded on three sides.'

'You can't be surrounded on three sides,' Rosanna jumped up impatiently. 'That means you're not surrounded.'

'I can see the wizard and Henry and the cannon!' shouted Kitty.

They could see the scene in the trees quite clearly now that the break in the Washer's line had caused a gap.

'We must run through the gap!' Mary leapt to her pink plastic feet.

The girls had never run so fast in their lives. Their hearts pounded, their legs ached, their wet hair whipped across their faces. Algie, half-hopping, half flying with his still sodden wings, had trouble keeping up with them.

'Wizard! Henry!' They shouted, 'We're coming! We're coming!'

The nearer the girls got to the barrage of mud balls the less they had to fear from the Washers. They sped past them, eyes blind and mouths agape with terror. They did have something to fear from the mud balls. A centre hit would have put any of them out of action.

But they didn't think of that. Another twenty or thirty yards and they would be out of the Washers' territory, safe beside the cannon. Already they could see the wizard and Henry jumping up and down and cheering.

'My heart is bursting,' panted Mary.

'Dolls don't have hearts,' panted Kitty.

'Of course they do. You just can't see them. Actually they're much bigger than . . .'

'Save your breath for running,' advised Rosanna. 'Not much further.'

Twenty more yards and about thirty terrified Washers between them and safety. It seemed as if they had won. Then a terrible thing happened. At first, they hardly noticed it. The pounding of their hearts had been the loudest sound for some time. Then they realised, they were not ducking or weaving anymore. No more cannon balls were thundering over their heads. Almost as soon as they realised it, the Washers did too. Their flight in the opposite direction slowed down and stopped. Although they were still frightened of the mud lying on the ground, they were no longer terror-stricken.

'What's happened?' shouted Rosanna despairingly.

THE GREAT BATTLE

What had happened was this. The wizard suspected it immediately and sent Henry off to the pond. The hose had fed mud from the pond down into the cannon at a tremendous speed. Eventually, the wet mud had been used up and the hose had reached the rocky bottom of the pond. Instead of stopping or sucking up water which would have given a warning, its power was so great that it had simply drawn on the first moveable rock. Although this had slid through the mouthpiece alright and even along the hose it had become blocked at the entrance to the cannon. Meanwhile, before the wizard could take steps to put that right, the hose had continued to suck up more and more rocks until it became entirely jammed.

Now the wizard was desperately trying to get out the first big rock and Henry, puffing like his own train, was attempting to move the hose to a muddier part of the pond.

The wizard's job was the easier. It would have needed a team of Nazrats to move the hose laden with so many rocks. Henry croaked to the wizard, 'I can't move it a centimetre.'

The wizard, struggling with the blocked bag, didn't answer. Then there was a sudden crash, the bag popped open and a huge stone crashed out — knocking over the wizard. He lay winded on the ground, arms and legs waving pathetically.

That was not all. As soon as the rock had jumped out, the bag snapped shut again to the cannon's end and with a noise greater than anything they had heard before, the cannon resumed firing.

But this time it was firing rocks. A steady stream of filthy, messy, wormy rocks crashed out from its barrel. After its initial mistake with the large rock, the hose mouth estimated the sizing perfectly and they slid along as easily as real cannon balls.

The tables were turned yet again. The wizard got up triumphantly. The Washers were on the run and the girls were free. They sped over the last few yards to the cannon and dropped onto the grass, shaking with exhaustion. It was a great reunion and the wizard allowed himself a rare smile at their congratulations.

'I'm so glad we didn't hit any of you,' he said very nicely.

The only note of discord came from Henry who had apparently expected them to bring the sandwiches.

They didn't even bother to watch the Washers retreat very clearly. If they had, they might have noticed a most disconcerting turn of events. The rocks, when they hit the ground, did not roll a little way and then lie still, as the mud balls had. They forced a hole through the grass and earth into which they disappeared. Completely. As if the hole was very deep. Each rock ball left a very

157

deep black hole.

Soon an even more disconcerting thing began to happen. Round objects began to shoot up out of the holes. They were not the rocks returning. They were something else. They were much bigger. At least they began the same size or they wouldn't have fitted into the holes but once they were out they seemed to swell until they were the size of a round television set. Secondly, they were coloured.

It was growing dark now. The sun had been gone for some time and the green tinge of the Washer territory was deepening into the blue of approaching night.

Kitty shivered. Mary yawned. They suddenly realised they were damp. They were cold. They were tired.

'I'm glad we don't have to start a battle now,' said Kitty. 'Aren't you Rosanna?'

Rosanna didn't answer. She was staring at something over her shoulder. She glanced at the wizard. He was looking the same way. He caught her eye.

'The Bouncers,' he said quietly.

'Come to support the Washers.'

Everybody else stopped talking and looked in the same direction. They saw a dozen or so huge balls, bouncing among the trees. Even in the gloom, their purple and pink and green and orange colours glowed weirdly. It would have only taken a couple of bouncers to crush the whole of the Right Side.

'I'll turn off the cannon before it makes any more holes,' the wizard's voice sounded choked.

'When we were inside their world you told me they would never hurt a human on purpose,' Rosanna tried not to panic.

'Unless the Washers have persuaded them,' the wizard

finished turning off the cannon and straightening up.

They all looked again. The balls seemed to be bouncing in a haphazard way. Forward and back. Side to side with no particular pattern. Certainly they were not advancing.

A more sinister sight appeared behind them. The Washers had reformed and were approaching at a purposeful march.

'I can't risk turning on the cannon,' said the wizard.

No-one answered. Although they knew he was right. There seemed nothing to be said. And not much to be done. It all depended on which way the Bouncers bounced.

They didn't have to wait long to find out. As the Washer Army came level with the huge coloured balls, a change came over them. They no longer bounced without order. Suddenly, they had formed into a line and were bouncing up and down in unison. Up all together to exactly the same height and down all together. As they hit the ground, Rosanna heard for the first time the horrid squeaking she remembered from her visit to their world.

There was no doubt this was a Bouncer army lined up and ready to go. Worse still, as the Washers caught up with them it was obvious where they were going. Towards the Right Side.

'They've joined the Wrong Side,' whispered Kitty.

'It's because they're so stupid,' said the wizard gloomily. No-one thought that much of a consolation.

Up and down. Up and down. Squeak. Squeak. The Bouncers advanced. Behind them marched the Washers. Ugh. Ugh. Ugh. Squeak. Grunt. Squeak. Grunt. It was quite a funny noise but no-one laughed.

'Excuse me.' They all turned round at the very humble voice of Algie eagle. 'I think it just possible that I may be dry enough to fly now. I may be able to get help . . .'

Poor Algie. He was so terrified of failing again. But in fact it was only a matter of seconds before he was off the ground and circling above their heads.

'He might bring some food,' said Henry.

Everybody looked at him with disgust.

It was now so dark that they could only see the lightest colours on the balls and the luminous green hair of the Washers. It looked very odd marching along without any body underneath.

It was fat Henry who had the first clever idea for some time. 'Has anyone got a pin?' he asked in his squeaky voice. Several pairs of eyes turned on him coldly. They were surprised he dared speak after his last ridiculous remark.

'I think there's a safety-pin in the hem of my dress.' Kitty took pity on him, 'Where Mummy never has time to sew it up.'

'Anything sharp and pointed would do,' squeaked Henry.

'What for?' asked the wizard.

'To pop the Bouncers,' said Henry in a matter of fact voice. 'They look like balloons. And they must be like them too because they swelled up more when they got out of the holes.'

'It's worth trying,' decided the wizard, after a moment's thought. 'Although they seem much heavier than something filled with air.'

'Anything's worth trying,' said Rosanna who found it very difficult to believe Henry could have had a good idea.

'Hand over pens, pins and any pointed objects,' commanded the wizard.

At that moment there was a flurry over their heads and a large dark shape followed by a much smaller, paler one, landed on the grass beside them.

'It's Algie,' exclaimed Mary in a disappointed voice.

'I'm sorry,' he began at once, 'but the cherub insisted on coming so I had to show her the way.'

There was a giggle from behind his broad back and the cherub fluttered out. She put her fingers in her mouth and blew out her chubby cheeks.

'This is no place for babies,' said the wizard severely.

The cherub held her fingers just outside her mouth and giggled again. 'Who saved Rosanna from the man-eating flowers?'

'Actually,' piped up Henry, 'Algie and the cherub could be very useful puncturing the Bouncers. They wouldn't risk being squashed if they do it from the air. Algie has a very sharp beak.'

It had to be admitted that Henry had come up with another good idea. Just in time too as the Bouncer army was almost on top of them.

'I love popping things!' cried the cherub when the plan had been explained. They all lined up, ready for a charge.

Only Rosanna remained reflective, 'Even if we pop all the Bouncers we've still got the Washers to deal with,' she said to herself because no-one else would listen. 'And it wasn't the cherub who actually saved me from the Man-Eating flowers, it was Nazrat.'

Perhaps this thought was suggested by a strange shaking in the trees high above the Washer Army's heads. But since no-one was listening they didn't notice that either.

They were off! Racing bravely to the great squeaking Bouncers. Armed with pins, sharp stones, beaks and bits of the cannon, they were a very weird army indeed.

The first victory went to Algie. His beak sank deep into the side of the leading Bouncer. There was a long drawn out squeal and the proud purple ball began to deflate. Out of its side oozed the most revolting green slime. It spread along the grass drawing the limp rubber down with it like a bit of dirty rag. 'It works!' screamed Algie. In ten seconds, he punctured as many Bouncers.

His was the most spectacular success but the others weren't doing badly. The little cherub, darting in with a safety pin caused particular havoc because the Bouncers could never guess where she was coming from. The wizard had devised a method of throwing a nail from the cannon, like an arrow.

Only fat Henry stood on the sidelines. But since the attack had been his idea no-one minded. Besides, they were a little worried that if he took part in the fight he might become muddled up with the Bouncers and get a nasty prick in his tummy. His round form and his squeaky voice made him too like them for safety. It was Henry who called out after ten minutes of squealing and bursting and oozing, 'Only two more Bouncers to go! And look what's happening now!'

Leaving the eagle to pop the last two which he did with ease and satisfaction, the others looked.

'They're going back down the holes,' cried Rosanna, 'what an extraordinary sight.'

'Revolting,' shuddered Kitty.

The rubbery remains of the Bouncers were oozing across the grass on a river of green slime. As each neared a hole they moved faster and then disappeared down it with a sudden pop as if sucked in by some strong internal pressure. A moment later the hole closed and the ground looked as if it had never been disturbed.

'Gone home,' said Henry proudly. 'Defeated. Vanquished. Conquered . . . Destroyed. *Veni. Vidi. Vici.*'

'What's that?' asked Rosanna.

'Latin. I came. I saw. I conquered.'

'I don't mean that. I mean up in the trees above the Washers.'

'The Washers!' Kitty stopped smiling. So did the others. In their excitement over beating the Bouncer Army, they had forgotten the Washer Army, lined up behind. Now they all strained their eyes in the direction of the rows of luminous green hair. Already they were starting to move forward, their stick legs beating time to their ugly grunts.

'I'm too tired for another battle,' said Kitty sinking to her knees.

'Watch the trees!' whispered Rosanna. As she spoke the leaves above the Washers' heads burst open and a line of large bodies swinging like spiders from the end of plaited vines swished towards them. The force of their descent was terrific. The noise as their rigid legs made contact with a Washer was delightful. Each swinging body knocked over a whole line of Washers in one swoop. Then it returned to the tree and prepared for another descent.

'Nazrat!' exulted Rosanna.

'And Friends,' said Algie, looking as nearly unhumble as he ever could. 'I did mention there might be a scrap if he was in the mood.'

163

'Oh Algie! So it's all your doing!'

'You're a bird in a million!'

Algie ducked his beaky head under his wing with the embarrassment of so much unaccustomed praise.

Seeing Nazrat and friends needed no help, the Right Side sat down thankfully on the grass. It was lovely to be watching someone else fighting.

'It's better than the Royal Tournament,' said the wizard.

'Better than television,' said Kitty.

'Except they've no sweets,' said Henry regretfully.

Since Nazrat and his friends took a line of Washers at a time it wasn't long before the whole Washer Army lay unconscious in neat rows. The victorious Nazrat swung towards the Right Side and landed on his two tree-trunk strong legs in front of them.

With one hand he held on to the end of the vine and with the other he beat his barrel chest. 'Glad to be of service,' he boomed.

One by one, they shook his hand and wished him a good journey home.

'I hear you're off to visit the Queen?'

'Yes, yes!' agreed Rosanna eagerly. 'On the top of

Hampstead Hill. Through the Golden Door.'

'You're on the right road then. I can't keep my men waiting any longer but if you like we'll give you a lift past the Washer territory. Not that they'll give you any more trouble.'

'Wheeeeeooooooo!' They all jumped as Nazrat put his finger in his mouth and blew a shrill whistle.

In two seconds a row of huge loin-cloth clad men stood in front of them. In another two seconds they found themselves swung high onto strong shoulders.

'My cannon!' cried the wizard, just in time. And that too found a bearer.

Then they were riding high through the dark green night, stepping over the rows of unconscious Washers, passing under the too green leaves and out into open grassland where the sky glittered with stars. There was a moon, too, giving enough light to see where they were going. Not that any one of the Right Side were much interested in looking. It was enough to be secure and riding comfortably towards their destination. The swaying movement was something like a camel, Rosanna imagined, head lolling.

'Hampstead Hill,' Nazrat said. He lowered Rosanna who he was carrying gently onto the ground. 'We turn off here. You must go on. It isn't far. Soon it will be dawn.'

'Dawn,' murmured Rosanna sleepily. Looking up she was just in time to see the moon disappear behind a neat round hill directly ahead. The stars were already so pale she could hardly see them. She realised she must have fallen asleep and they had travelled a long distance.

Around her Nazrat's men were setting down the others who stumbled dazedly and rubbed their eyes as if they also had been asleep. By the time they'd recovered Nazrat had gone and they were on their own again.

They gathered together, shivering in the pre-dawn cool. Rosanna pointed up the hill, 'That's where we're going,' she said. 'Hampstead Hill, Nazrat said.'

'To the top,' the wizard nodded sleepily.

The top of the hill was covered with a thick mist. As the sun rose behind it, it began to be tinged with yellow.

'I think there might be a building on it. A white building,' said Rosanna slowly.

'I'm tired,' said Kitty in a small voice.

'I'm hungry,' said Henry in a small squeak. However this turned into a big squeak as the brightening light showed up a basket set at his feet. 'The sandwiches!'

'They must have collected them for us on the way,' said the wizard, with just as greedy an expression as Henry.

There was no doubt that the hill looked much smaller after a breakfast of cheddar cheese sandwiches.

They set off in fine pacing style with Algie and the cherub circling round them like escorting helicopters. Soon the rays from the still hidden sun had burnt off the mist and they could see quite clearly a large white building sitting on the top of the hill. As they drew nearer it seemed that the light came not from the sun but from the building itself. It shone so brightly that they could hardly bear to look at it.

Soon they were within the courtyard and shielding their eyes with their hands so as not to be blinded saw in the centre of the building a gleaming golden door.

'We've got to go through that,' cried Rosanna, her head throbbing as if with sunstroke.

She moved forward slowly, arms outstretched now as if to touch the door. Though she was afraid, too, that it might be burning hot like the sun.

At last she was right in front of it. But the brilliance was unbearable.

She shut her eyes and put both hands up to her face. But the light was so bright that it seemed to shine right through them. She squeezed her eyes tighter and a million sparks of colour flew and danced. She felt as if she was blinded and her head close to bursting.

She took her hands from her face and held them out once more in front of her. She was certain that if she could only touch the door, the unbearable brightness would disappear and she would find the Queen's peace. Using all her will-power, she struggled to take a step forward. But the light seemed to have struck through her and fixed her to the ground.

'Oh Queen!' she cried out, 'oh beautiful Queen, oh Legless Queen! Please help me come to you!'

THROUGH THE GOLDEN DOOR

Rosanna didn't know it at the time but everyone of the Right Side was going through the same experience. They all stood with their eyes squeezed shut, transfixed to the ground by the brilliantly shining door. They all saw bright dashes and flashes of colour. They all prayed for rescue.

'What are you waiting for?' cried a voice from behind the door, 'aren't you coming *in*?'

'The Queen!' rejoiced Rosanna. And in a second they had all pushed through the door and burst into the bedroom.

Immediately they were surrounded by warmth and light (a soft pink light) and colour. Flowers were everywhere, roses, lupins, peonies, daisies, marigolds, pansies, lavender, clarkia, carnations, chrysanthemums, sweet peas and huge while lilies standing like sentinels at either side of the bed.

And there sat the Queen, more beautiful than ever, her lustrous dark hair plaited with silver and white ribbons, her shoulders draped in folds of creamy lace

168

and her usual escort of brilliantly coloured butterflies flickering around her.

'Greenhouses unlimited, what a crowd!' she cried raising one ringed hand to her forehead. 'It's lucky I'm feeling so well or I might turn the lot of you out *toute de suite*.'

'*Tout* what?' asked Rosanna forgetting her nervousness

'She means *immediately*!' bellowed a huge voice. And there was the King eagle seated on a chair with his usual glass of wine and half-read newspaper.

'Ssshh, my regal eagle,' said the Queen, smiling sweetly, 'as I said, I'm in such a good mood that I wouldn't dream of turning anyone out. Especially not these modern day Argonauts. Mary?' she stopped for a moment, 'I presume Mary is here?'

'Oh, yes, Queen!'

'Quite, my bakelite poppet. Serve champagne at once. My dear Kingy has popped the tops. Now don't you all want to see!'

'See what?'

Rosanna's voice landed into a sudden silence. The Queen sat up straight, peered at her and then fell back among the pillows as if amazed.

'See what?' she muttered, 'see what? If it wasn't the little sugar-plum (with ugly knickers) speaking I don't know what I'd do.' She suddenly came bolt upright again. 'See *him*, of course!' she cried. 'That's what you're all here for isn't it?'

Him? Rosanna tried to see between the curtain of flowers and butterflies.

'Him!' repeated the Queen even louder. And then a very amazing thing happened. For the legless Queen got out of her bed and walked over to Rosanna. Rosanna felt an arm round her shoulders and she was drawn over towards the far side of the bed.

'Him,' said the Queen yet again but this time in an extra special gentle voice. 'The baby.'

And there in a cot draped in white silk patterned with the smallest of little red hearts, lay a tiny dark-haired baby. 'Charming, don't you think?' said the Queen taking Rosanna's finger and stroking it against the baby's soft cheek. 'On balance worth the wait.'

'Oh, yes,' breathed Rosanna who felt quite awestruck by the occasion. But her peaceful admiration was interrupted by the most piercing noise in her right ear. The cherub was blowing her trumpet.

'Zoe, bubble,' sighed the Queen with surprising patience. She winked an eye at Rosanna. 'Jealous,' she mouthed. 'Jasper will just have to get used to it.'

'Jasper?' repeated Rosanna looked at the cradle worriedly. She wasn't sure such a little creature deserved quite such a — well — individual name. But as she looked she was diverted by an odd movement from the cradle. The cradle itself, that is, not the baby.

It was beginning to rock, being pushed. Quite fast. Backwards and forwards.

'Oh!' The Queen turned at her gasp. Just in time to see a black figure with a tall pointed hat creep out from under the cot.

'Not bad,' said the wizard, unfolding to his full height. He stood back and looked at the cradle which was rocking so fiercely that the baby was rolling from side to side. 'A mechanical device. Not bad at all for a spur of the moment invention. It does six tilts a second, though if I changed the gear synchronisation mechanism I could probably raise that to ten.'

170

'Bustling Begonias, No!' said the Queen hastily as the wizard seemed ready to dive back under the cradle again. 'Six tilts is ample. In fact if you could slow it down to two or three dear little Jasper would enjoy it even more.'

Rosanna thought it remarkable that dear little Jasper wasn't awake and screaming what with the cherub's continuing trumpet blasts and the gale force motion he was enduring. Personally, she wanted to take him out of the cot and give him a good quiet cuddle. But she didn't dare ask.

She looked at the Queen who had left the baby (now being geared down to two tilts a second) and was climbing with remarkable agility for someone with no legs back into bed. Rosanna noticed she was still smiling. That was remarkable too when you considered what a disorderly rumpus was going on round her.

The King eagle was serving champagne in tall crystal glasses. Algie was sipping politely but every now and again he gave a loud hiccough. After each hiccough he apologized profusely.

Kitty with a large goblet in her hand, was behaving badly. She had discovered that if she held the champagne out to the lilies they bent right over and the long yellow tongues inside their horns uncurled for a sip. This, combined with the fizzy champagne, had given her the giggles which, despite all Mary's banging on her back, had made her do the nose-trick. She was not at all a respectable sight.

Henry who, surprisingly, thought champagne 'beastly stuff' was more sober. He had discovered the old fashioned gramophone, and was winding the golden handle. Soon the cherub's trumpet was accompanied by a jazz arrangement of 'Happy Birthday' followed by a solo rendering of 'When Day is Done'.

'Paralysed Peonies!' shouted the Queen. She had to shout to make herself heard above the racket. 'You know what would really please me!'

Rosanna knew it at once. But before she could say anything it had started all on its own.

> *'God Save our Lovely Queen*
> *God Save our Legless Queen . . .'*

the gramophone roared out. And although the words didn't sound quite as usual to Rosanna she was much too concerned to hear if it went on to the second and third verses to worry.

'Make her luxurious
Happily riproarious
Long to reign over us
God Save our Queen!'

It was just then that Rosanna heard a new noise. A high-pitched wail something like Henry's train whistle. Gradually she realised it was coming from the two-tilts-a-second-cradle. She looked at the Queen but she was far too busy enjoying her song to be listening for her baby. And everybody else was singing.

Rosanna went over to the cradle and peered in. Poor Jasper! Instead of looking like a curled up pink shell as he had before, now he was bright red and his mouth was wide open. Rosanna would never have guessed he could have such a big mouth nor that he could make so much noise.

Very carefully, she lifted him out of the cradle and supporting his wobbly head with one arm carried him to a low velvet covered chair by the bed. To her delight, he immediately stopped crying and his face resumed its previous shape and colour.

She felt very content sitting on the little chair with the warm baby in her arms. She was sheltered from the wild noise and activity of the rest of the room by the high bed. She even forgot to listen for the second and third verses of 'God Save Our Queen'.

When the chair began to rock gently, she didn't question it at all. Either it was a rocking chair or the wizard had re-positioned his invention. Either way it was most agreeable. Although it did make her feel very sleepy.

Oh dear. Rosanna jerked her eyes open. It would be terrible to fall asleep and let Jasper roll off her lap. But it really was becoming harder and harder to stay awake.

Her last memory, coming to her through waves of sleep were the final bellowed lines of 'God Save Our Queen'.

'It's tea-time!'

'It's tea-time' was a line Rosanna heard every day of her life. But on this occasion it sounded quite extraordinary to her. It was shouted by her brother, Mat.

'It's tea-time! Lazy-bones!' This was not particularly odd either. He was quite often sent to fetch her. And usually followed up the information by some insult.

Tea-time. Rosanna tried to think why it seemed such an odd idea. It might help if she opened her eyes. For once Mat was quite right to call her lazy-bones. He was stalking back into the house. He was probably in a hurry to eat his tea and start making some noisy model.

She was sitting on the swing. It still moved gently as if she had been pushing it with her feet even when asleep. Why was tea-time so odd? Champagne! The word popped into her head. They had been drinking champagne. That was a clue. But where? Why were dreams so difficult to remember? Dreams? Was it only dreams?

A baby! A Queen's baby. A Queen who had a baby. If she could just hold on to that she might remember more.

'You've got to come in at once!' Zoe stood in front of her. By her round tummy Rosanna guessed she had

174

already eaten her tea.

'You interrupted me!'

'What?' Zoe widened her eyes sympathetically.

'Now I'll never remember,' Rosanna resisted the urge to give Zoe a pinch. 'I had such an exciting dream.'

'I dreamt I fell over. Did you too?'

'Oh, no! It was much more exciting than that.' Rosanna stood up regretfully, 'What's for tea?'

'Burnt sausages.'

'Again'. Rosanna followed the round figure and bouncing yellow curls towards the house. When she reached the door a surprising thought came to her, 'I suppose Mummy hasn't had the baby by any chance,' she said almost to herself.

'Oh, no!' Zoe turned round and put her fingers in her mouth which she did whenever there was any mention of the baby. 'The baby's coming on Sunday.'

'Do you think so.' Zoe only knew the word for Sunday so everything was expected to happen on that day. Rosanna sighed. The smell of burnt sausages was very strong. It wasn't that she didn't like them. It was just that it was boring having them every day.

She turned round and gave one last look to the garden. The sun had moved along its length as she slept. Now there was only a thin strip on the very end. As she watched it blinked and went out. Now the sun passed right over their garden and lit up the blue evening sky. It also shone on a high window in the back of the tall row of houses beyond their garden wall. Rosanna had never particularly noticed the window before but now it seemed familiar, more than that, important. Something to do with her dreams.

'Come on, lazy-toes!' called Zoe, dragging at her hand.

It was no good. The sun merely bounced off the glass. She could never see inside. Besides, now she looked more, it really was a perfectly ordinary London house window.

'I'm coming,' she gave Zoe's plump hand a squeeze.

'Mama's baby *will* come on Sunday,' Zoe gave a skip. 'A bird told me. A great big eagle.'

'An eagle?' Rosanna stopped for one more second. But then she was in the kitchen and quite surrounded by the smell of burnt sausages.

'Bustling begonias! I'm hungry!' She was too busy eating to wonder where she'd picked up such an unusual expression.